★ American Girl®

D0029732

TENNEY
Shares the Stage

by **Kelle**n Her**t**z

Scholastic Inc.

Published by Scholastic Inc., *Publishers since 1920.* SCHOLASTIC and associated logos are trademarks and/or registered trademarks of Scholastic Inc. The publisher does not have any control over and does not assume any responsibility for author or third-party websites or their content.

This book is a work of fiction. Names, characters, places, and incidents are either the product of the author's imagination or are used fictitiously, and any resemblance to actual persons, living or dead, business establishments, events, or locales is entirely coincidental and not intended by American Girl or Scholastic Inc.

Cover illustration by Juliana Kolesova
Author photo credit, p. 199: Sonya Sones

americangirl.com/service

ISBN 978-1-338-11757-8

10 9 8 7 6 5 4 3 2 1   17 18 19 20 21

Printed in China 62 • First printing 2017

For John—
I love sharing our song with you.

CONTENTS

A NEW SOUND

Chapter 1

I always feel the same when I'm reaching the end of a performance: My feet feel like rocks from standing while holding my guitar, my fingers ache from picking strings, the back of my neck's sweaty under my leather neck strap . . . and I'm in heaven. That's how I felt as Logan Everett and I played the last song of our set in the amphitheater at Cumberland Park.

As I sang, I scanned the crowd clustered on the wide lawn around the stage. We were playing as part of a one-day music festival to raise money for Nashville's parks. I'd been to concerts here, but never as a performer. Now, with the stage solid under my boots, I felt proud of how far I had come.

A few months ago, I'd only daydreamed about performing my own songs in concert. When I told my parents I wanted to get serious about starting a career in music, they said I was too young. But with a combination of hard work and good timing, I managed to convince them that I was ready. I also caught the attention of Zane Cale, a producer at Mockingbird Records, who thought I had a lot of potential and wanted to become my manager. At first I was super excited, but then Zane decided that my songs would be even better if I was playing them with Logan, a fourteen-year-old drummer with a ton of talent—and an ego to match. Needless to say, we were still getting used to being partners. But as I watched the heads bobbing to our music, I couldn't help feeling that I had ended up in the right place.

This was the largest audience we'd ever played for—even bigger than the enormous crowd that had shown up for our concert at Dad's store last month in response to pop singer Belle Starr's social media posts about Logan and me. Today's turnout was so big because a lot of bands were playing after us at the festival, but, strangely, I wasn't nervous. Instead, looking across the sea

A NEW SOUND

of shining faces, I felt as if I was made of light. Up above, the clouds in the bright blue sky seemed to bounce to our music.

With a flourish on my guitar and a final crash of Logan's cymbals, our song ended. For a moment, the whole world took a breath. Then an explosion of applause nearly knocked me off my feet. I felt dizzy, like I'd just stepped off a merry-go-round.

"Thank you, Nashville!" I said into the mic.

"Yes!" Logan chimed in from behind his drum set. "We are Logan and Tenney!"

I wrinkled my nose. When Zane had signed us to a recording contract as a duo, he'd told us we needed to come up with an official band name. We'd decided to keep it simple and stick with Tenney & Logan. But for some reason, Logan always put *his* name first.

"We're also Tenney and Logan," I added jokingly. The crowd laughed. "Thanks so much for listening!" I said.

Logan stuck his drumsticks in his back pocket and slipped around his drum kit to join me as we took our bows.

TENNEY SHARES THE STAGE

"Good set," I whispered to him as we made our way offstage.

Logan shrugged. "We could have been snappier on 'Reach the Sky,'" he replied.

I felt a nip of annoyance but tried to ignore it. Since I'd started playing with Logan, I'd learned that he often focused more on what was wrong than on what was right.

"We sounded good," I insisted as we jostled down the side steps behind the stage. "You're just mad because I wouldn't pick up the tempo."

Logan cracked a smile. "You're right," he admitted.

"I know," I said with a wink.

Ever since we'd signed our contract, Logan and I had been rehearsing twice a week. Usually, we got along, but we still clashed sometimes. In rehearsal, Logan often tried new things midsong without warning me, which drove me crazy, and he hated it when I insisted we practice a song until it was perfect. Still, when we really listened to each other, there was no question that we rocked.

"Tenney! Logan!"

A NEW SOUND

I turned around. My little sister, Aubrey, rushed up in an excited whirl of pink sparkles. "You were awesome!" she squeaked, giving me a hug.

"Thanks," I said.

"But wasn't something missing from your show?" she asked playfully.

Logan's eyebrows shot up in surprise. "Missing?" he asked.

"Like what?" I asked.

"Like *me*, on accordion!" Aubrey proclaimed. "I've been practicing a lot, and I'm getting really good."

"You are," I admitted. Everyone in my family plays an instrument or two, and even though Aubrey's only seven, she's got some mean accordion skills.

"So can I back you guys up in your next show?" Aubrey begged, giving us her best hopeful puppy-dog look. Logan and I exchanged a glance.

"It's not really that simple," I pointed out gently. "We'd have to ask Mom and Dad, and Zane . . ."

"Oh," Aubrey said, starting to wilt.

"But it's not impossible," Logan added, with an

encouraging smile. "Just keep practicing, and we'll see what happens."

Aubrey hugged him with a squeal. Logan looked startled, as if he'd just been attacked by an overexcited baby bear. I had to laugh.

As Logan gently loosened Aubrey's grip, Zane bounded up to us like a jackrabbit, grinning from ear to ear.

"There's the dynamic duo!" he said to us. "Great set! Keep that up, and I can see a Tenney and Logan record in your future."

"Really?" I said, excitement pulsing through me. A *record* of my own music! It was something I'd dreamed of for as long as I could remember.

"Well, we need to keep building your songwriting," said Zane. "But you guys definitely have the musical chops and the onstage chemistry."

"When you *do* start recording," Aubrey told Zane, "I'd be willing to guest-star on a track if you need an accordion."

"Good to know," Zane told her with a wink. Aubrey looked thrilled as Zane turned to Logan. "Is your mom around?"

A NEW SOUND

Logan shook his head. "She had to work at the last minute."

"Okay," Zane said. "Well, I've got something to discuss with y'all. Let's go find Tenney's parents."

We followed him around the back of the amphitheater up to the main entrance. Out front, several food trucks sat in a row in the parking lot. My mom's sky-blue truck was smack in the middle, its chrome hubcaps as shiny as mirrors. GEORGIA'S GENUINE TENNESSEE HOT CHICKEN was stenciled across the side in red cursive letters.

As we got closer, Dad stuck his head out of the truck's service window and waved to us. He owns a music store in East Nashville, where we live, but he helps Mom out with her truck when he can. "Hey, Georgia, the Gruesome Twosome is back!" he called to my mom inside the truck. "How's that for a band name, Tenn?"

I grinned. "I think we'll stick with Tenney and Logan for now."

Mom opened the truck's back door. "Hey there!" she greeted us, sweeping some loose tendrils of carrot-red hair back under her bandanna.

"From in here, you two sounded great."

"I think they could use some accordion," Aubrey said.

"Glad to know you have an opinion, Aubrey," Dad joked.

Before I could say anything, Logan broke in. "Are you guys done serving for the day?" he asked my parents.

"For the most part," Mom replied. "Lunch rush is over."

Logan looked crushed. "Does that mean you're out of hot chicken?"

"I didn't say *that*," Mom said, putting a hand on her hip. "I thought you two might be hungry, so I saved you some."

Logan's eyes brightened. "Thanks!"

We sat behind the food truck on folding chairs, at the card table Mom always sets up for a rest area. Dad brought everyone watermelon lemonades as Mom served up brown-paper trays of hot chicken, cheddar biscuits, and slices of watermelon. Logan dug in like he hadn't eaten in days. I drained my lemonade, realizing how thirsty I was after singing.

A NEW SOUND

"Y'all should be proud of yourselves," Zane said to Logan and me. He leaned back in his chair, pushing the worn porkpie hat he always wore off his face. "The more shows you play together, the better you sound."

"Thanks," I replied, pleased. We'd played four shows in the past month. I thought we'd been sounding great, but I hadn't wanted to seem like a show-off by saying it out loud.

"When are we going to start booking some *paid* gigs?" Logan asked.

"Soon, I hope," Zane replied. "But remember, you're just starting out. We're going to have to play at least *some* shows for free as the Nashville music community gets more familiar with who y'all are. Then, once we've built a loyal fan base, we can book more paid club gigs. Does that make sense?"

I nodded, but Logan's mouth twisted into an uncertain knot. "I guess so," he said at last.

"Good," Zane said. "But there's something even more important we need to focus on. You two need to start building your own musical style together, as Tenney and Logan."

I scrunched up my nose. "I don't understand; you just said we sounded great."

I already worked really hard to find my own voice, I thought to myself. *Can't Logan just adapt to my style?*

"You *do* sound great," Zane said, looking from me to Logan. "You guys are a solid team musically, but to have a professional career you need to be more than solid—you need to be distinctive. That means having a unique sound. To get there, you need to be writing songs *together.*"

Logan and I both went silent. I wasn't surprised by Zane's suggestion. After all, bands write songs together all the time. But the thought of writing a song from scratch with Logan made me nervous. I already *had* a sound as a songwriter, and I liked it. The few songs I'd heard that Logan had written were harder rock 'n' roll than what I liked. On top of this, when Logan and I had worked together on my song "Where You Are," we'd bickered all the time about our musical opinions. Wouldn't that only get worse if we were writing together? Just thinking about it made my head hurt.

Logan seemed to be reading my mind.

A NEW SOUND

"I write better alone," he told Zane.

"Me, too," I said, relieved.

The adults gave us skeptical looks.

"It's true," I insisted.

"I'm sure it is right *now*," Zane said lightly. "But you don't climb a mountain by going around it."

"I couldn't agree more," Dad chimed in as Mom nodded.

"You two are musical partners on stage and off," she added. "A huge part of what makes a band successful is having original music that's your own recognizable sound."

I knew they were right, but uncertainty was rising like a tidal wave in my stomach. I love writing songs by myself. For me, it's something private and thoughtful that I do to figure out my emotions, like writing in a diary. Thinking about having to share that with Logan Everett made me want to curl up in a ball. But I couldn't tell him that. I racked my brain for another reason that would convince Zane that this was a bad idea.

"I'm not really used to writing to a drumbeat—" I began, but Zane cut in.

TENNEY SHARES THE STAGE

"Logan plays bass and guitar, too," he pointed out, "so it shouldn't be hard for you two to collaborate on melodies."

He was right, of course. Most musicians start writing a song using a guitar or a piano. Since Logan played, too, I knew we'd be *able* to collaborate. I just wasn't feeling too excited about it. From his expression, I could tell Logan wasn't, either.

"I guess," he said, as if he had just agreed to take out the trash.

"I still don't understand," I said. "Why can't we just write on our own and bring songs in when they're done?"

"You can," Zane said evenly. "But you also need to get in a room and make some new music together. Look, I know it was rough when y'all collaborated on 'Where You Are,' but it turned out so good because you each brought something different to it," he noted. "The path's going to get smoother as you two get to know each other better musically."

Logan and I shared a glance. He looked as uneasy as I felt.

A NEW SOUND

"I just think we're so different; I'm worried we won't agree on anything," I said.

"I agree!" Logan said, nodding.

"See? You just agreed on something," Zane pointed out.

We both started protesting, and Zane put up a hand to silence us, chuckling.

"Pipe down," he said gently. "I had a feeling that you two wouldn't be very happy about this. And I know that you both can be very stubborn when it comes to songwriting. That's why I asked Portia Burns if she'd oversee some songwriting sessions with you both, to start you off. Cool?"

I nodded as Logan did, and my stomach relaxed. Logan and I had worked with Portia before, and we both trusted her. She's been a songwriter and performer in Nashville since my mom was a kid. Plus, she's my friend. If anyone could keep me from walking out on Logan in the middle of a songwriting session, I thought, it was Portia.

"Glad you approve," Zane said, folding his arms behind his head again. His eyes twinkled reassuringly. "I'll stop by after you guys have met a couple of times to hear what you've cooked up. Once we build that unique Tenney and Logan sound into your songwriting, we can start putting together enough original songs for an EP."

Excitement vibrated through me. An EP is like a mini album—between three and five songs long—that bands record when they're just starting out, almost like a test run. If Zane was talking about letting Logan and me make an EP, I knew he definitely thought we had the potential to make it as professional musicians.

Logan's eyes were electric sparks, so I could tell he was excited, too.

"When do we start recording?" he asked Zane.

"Whoa, now," Zane cautioned. "We still have a ways to go before we book studio time. I need you guys focused on songwriting. You need to be rehearsing three times a week, plus working with Portia every week. We have a playing room at Mockingbird where you can practice."

"Okay," I said, my brain spinning. I looked at Logan. His face had darkened, and he was shaking his head.

A NEW SOUND

"I can't do that," he said. "I can only meet twice a week."

Zane's eyebrows shot up, but when he spoke his voice was mild. "This is a big opportunity for you, Logan," he said. "It requires a big commitment."

Logan stared at the table. It was tough to tell what he was thinking, but he didn't look happy.

"I can only do two times a week," he repeated, crumpling up his greasy napkin.

"Are you sure?" I asked.

"Yes," he growled, shooting me a look that dared me to say more. "And I can't rehearse at Mockingbird. It's too far from my house."

I blinked in disbelief. Logan seemed to be happiest when he was playing music. It seemed weird that he was being so grouchy about this.

Everyone sat there for an awkward moment.

"You live in Rosebank, right, Logan?" Mom said. "That's not too far from us. You two could rehearse at Tenney's dad's music shop."

"Sure, I have a small drum kit you could use during rehearsals," Dad added. "Would that work for you, Logan?"

TENNEY SHARES THE STAGE

Logan's expression softened a little, and he nodded. "I guess I could probably rehearse two times a week plus once a week with Portia," he mumbled.

"Sounds like a deal," Zane said. "Why don't you both take a couple of days to brainstorm song ideas, then meet on, say, Tuesday afternoon at the shop and start songwriting?"

I nodded thoughtfully. "Right, and then we could meet at Portia's after school on Thursday and play what we have."

Zane looked satisfied. "Excellent. I'll check with Portia to make sure that day will work for her. Does that sound good, Logan?"

Logan was checking his phone. "Sure," he said, standing up. "I have to go. Mom's picking me up at the side entrance."

"I'll walk you over there," I said, jumping up.

He moved so fast that I had to skip to keep up as we darted past food trucks toward a gated park entrance.

"Are you okay?" I asked.

"Yeah," he replied, but his voice sounded a hundred miles away.

A NEW SOUND

Maybe he's nervous about writing together, like I am,
I thought. "I know writing together won't be easy,
but I'm glad we're giving it a shot," I said, trying to
reassure myself as much as Logan. "Maybe Zane's
right. If we're going to be successful, we need to
have a distinctive sound. I think that if we keep—"

"Tenney, I get it," Logan snapped. "My dad's a
professional musician, remember? I know what it
takes to be successful."

Heat flooded my cheeks. *What is* with *him,
anyway?* I thought.

I could tell Logan knew he'd hurt my feelings.
"I'm sorry," he said, rubbing his eyes. "You're right.
I'm just tired."

We reached the side entrance. A green truck
was idling by the curb outside. Logan's mom was
behind the steering wheel in the fuchsia hospital
scrubs she usually had on the few times I'd seen
her. Mrs. Everett is a pediatric nurse. I knew she
worked a lot, but she was always super friendly,
even on the days when she seemed really tired.

"Hey, guys," she said with a wave. "How was
the show?"

"Great!" I said. Logan got into the truck as I told her about our set.

"Sounds like you two tore it up," Logan's mom said, grinning at him. "I wish I could've made it."

"Next time," I told her. She nodded.

"Mom, I'm late," he reminded her.

"I know," Mrs. Everett said mildly, and kissed him on the head. He looked beyond embarrassed.

"Bye, Tenney," Logan mumbled, and his mom waved again. As the truck pulled away, he threw a sneaky glance back at me, as if he was worried I'd follow him.

Weird, I thought. As I watched the truck turn the corner out of view, I realized that beyond music, there was a whole lot I didn't know about Logan Everett. Maybe that was why part of me still didn't quite trust him.

BE PROFESSIONAL

Chapter 2

*M*y friend Holliday stopped in the center of the school hallway and stared at me. "No way," she said, blue eyes wide. "You and Logan are going to make a record?"

"It's just an EP, and it's not going to happen for a long time," I said quickly. I didn't want to sound like I was bragging.

"Who cares *when* it happens?" my best friend, Jaya, squeaked. "It's amazing!"

"I know," I whispered. Seeing my friends bursting with pride made it all feel very real. A wave of joy surged through me and I did a happy twirl.

"Watch it!" said a passing eighth grader as I bumped into him.

"Oops! Sorry!" I called after him, but I couldn't stop grinning.

TENNEY SHARES THE STAGE

Holliday, Jaya, and I talked about the future Tenney & Logan EP all during lunch in the cafeteria.

"I know what's going to happen," Holliday said, dreaming out loud. "You and Logan will record the EP, and it'll be a huge hit and your career will take off!"

"She's right!" Jaya trilled. "I can help design the EP cover and your website ..."

"... And I'll organize your concert tour," Holliday finished.

"That would be great," I said with a smile. Jaya's a great artist, and Holliday loves planning events. Plus, her dad works for a record label, so she knows a lot about the music business. It was nice that they wanted to help out, but what meant the most was seeing how genuinely happy they were for me.

"Now all you guys have to do is decide which songs to record for the EP!" Holliday said.

I winced and nodded, glancing at the edge of my songwriting journal, which was peeking out of the top of my book bag. As I ran my hand along it, my floaty happiness evaporated into a flutter of nerves.

BE PROFESSIONAL

"What's wrong?" Jaya asked, cocking her head.

"Zane wants Logan and me to write some new songs together," I grumbled, taking a bite of my sandwich.

"But you love songwriting," Holliday chirped. "What do you have to be worried about? It'll be fun!"

I nearly choked on a bite of peanut butter and banana. "No," I said, after I'd managed to swallow. "It is *not* going to be fun."

Holliday and Jaya looked at me with matching furrowed brows.

"Logan and I have totally different personalities and tastes," I explained. "We got into so many arguments just working on 'Where You Are.' He's talented, but he's so stubborn."

"Like you," Jaya said with a grin.

"I'm not stubborn!" I protested. Then I realized how stubborn I sounded. "Fine," I admitted. "Maybe I am *sometimes*."

"Especially about your music!" Jaya said, letting out a giggle.

"That's because it's *my* music," I said

passionately. "I hear it in my head; I know the way it should be. Anything else just sounds wrong."

Holliday took a sip of her milk and squinted thoughtfully. "Even if you and Logan disagree on things, you sound great together onstage," she said. "Isn't that what's important?"

"That's part of it, but the songwriting's even more important, because it can decide our future as a duo," I explained. I let out a sigh. "If Logan and I can't learn to collaborate, this could turn into a musical disaster."

"Try to focus on the songs, not on Logan," Holliday advised.

"Easier said than done," I said. "I've been trying to brainstorm song ideas for my writing session with Logan today, but everything just seems wrong."

"I can help you!" Holliday said, her eyes crackling with enthusiasm.

"Me, too!" Jaya agreed.

"Really? Okay," I said, surprised at how relieved I felt. I pulled out my songwriting journal and fished a pen out of my bag. "I need to come

BE PROFESSIONAL

up with topics to write about, for a start."

"Everyone always writes about being in love, but music can be about so much more than that," Jaya offered. "You should write a song about helping the earth."

"Yes!" I said, cracking open my journal.

"There should be more songs about friendship, too," Holliday added. "And otters."

"Otters?" I said, a little confused.

Holliday nodded. "They're so cute," she said. "They deserve their own song."

"What about a song about how hard it is to get up on Monday mornings?" Jaya said.

"Good idea," I said, writing it down. "Everyone can relate to that."

By the time lunch was over, Jaya and Holliday had helped me come up with a long list of ideas for possible songs. I wasn't sure how many of them Logan would like, but *I* liked them. That was enough to make me happy.

TENNEY SHARES THE STAGE

When school ended, I walked over to Dad's music store. It's just a few blocks away, snuggled next to a pizzeria at the end of a long strip of brightly painted storefronts with big windows. As soon as I turned the corner, I could see the cheery wooden sign reading GRANT'S MUSIC AND COLLECTIBLES hanging over the entrance.

The cluttered little shop felt like a second home to me. I could describe it with my eyes closed. Its walls were decorated with album posters and covered from floor to ceiling with gleaming guitars, mandolins, and banjos that hung from hooks. The instruments' polished wood and metal bodies reflected the afternoon light, giving the place a magical glow. The air smelled like cedar and guitar glue.

Suddenly, a memory floated into my mind: I was a few years younger than Aubrey is now, running through the store. I stopped midstride and watched Dad tenderly hanging each instrument on the display wall as if it were a rare jewel. That very day I asked Dad to teach me how to play guitar. Coming back to reality, I felt all over again how much I love it here.

I spotted Logan through the shop's window. He was crouched on the small demo stage on the far side of the shop, setting up a drum kit. Dad stood over him, supervising. I wasn't exactly looking forward to our first songwriting session, but at least we were in my territory.

Here goes nothing, I thought to myself, and entered the store. As the front door jangled shut, they both saw me.

"Tennyson!" Dad said with a broad grin.

Logan gave me a curious look.

"Tennyson's my full name," I explained shyly.

"Correction!" Dad said. "Your full name is Tennyson Evangeline Grant. Named after the great poet, Alfred, Lord Tennyson."

My cheeks got hot. I like my full name, but it's a mouthful, and for a moment I was worried Logan might make a joke about it. To my relief, he went back to fastening the last cymbal onto its stand without a word.

"Looks good," Dad said, nodding. "And you need to borrow a guitar for songwriting, I assume."

"If that's okay," Logan said. "I don't own my own guitar yet."

"I've got a couple in here somewhere," Dad joked. He pulled a small-bodied acoustic off the wall and handed it to Logan.

"Thank you," Logan replied. "And thanks again for letting us practice here, Mr. Grant."

Dad waved a hand. "Of course," he replied. "We don't get many customers in here on weekday afternoons, and if we do, they'll be happy to hear some live music."

He turned to me. "I'm going to go do inventory in the stockroom. Y'all come get me if we get any customers or if you need anything." With that, he disappeared into the back.

I grabbed my guitar case from its place beneath the cash register and my songwriting journal from my bag, and we started tuning up. We didn't talk much, which was fine by me. I wondered how we'd decide who was right when Logan and I disagreed about something—because we were definitely going to disagree.

I started playing scales as I always did

before a songwriting session. Logan just sat
there, clicking around on his phone. *Doesn't
he need to warm up?* I thought. I let my gaze drift
down to the mother-of-pearl songbird inlaid
on my guitar. *Just focus on the music,* it seemed
to be telling me, echoing Holliday. I smiled to
myself. Warmth crept into my fingers as I picked
up my pace. After a few minutes, my hands felt
nimble, like if I let them go, they might twirl
into the sky.

"Ready," I said, glancing at Logan. He was
checking his cell phone. Annoyance buzzed
through me.

"Yeah," Logan said after a moment, as if he'd
just remembered we were supposed to be working.
He set down his phone.

"So I came up with some song ideas—" I began,
but Logan's phone chimed with a new text, cutting
me off.

"Hold on," he said. He checked his phone and
started typing. My feet did an impatient tap dance.
After what seemed like forever, the text sent with
a *whoosh* and Logan looked up.

TENNEY SHARES THE STAGE

"Maybe you could turn off your phone," I said.

Logan looked at me like I'd just grown a third eye. "No way," he replied.

"We're supposed to be working on song ideas," I said, an edge creeping into my voice.

Logan shrugged in that offhand way that drove me crazy. "Some things are more important," he said.

"Like your phone?" I snapped before I could stop myself.

Logan gave me a hard look, and for a moment, I had a flash of how I'd felt when we argued while we were working on "Where You Are."

"I'll turn off the ringer," he said at last.

"Thank you," I said, resisting the urge to roll my eyes.

I flipped through my journal, looking for the list that Jaya and Holliday had helped me brainstorm.

"I've been thinking a lot about friendship, and how important it is," I said. "That could make a good song."

Logan shrugged again. "It's pretty unoriginal."

BE PROFESSIONAL

"Unoriginal?" I said, feeling irritation start to bubble inside.

"Yeah, there are zillions of songs about friendship. And Zane said that we're supposed to write songs that are unique," Logan pointed out. "Plus, it's kind of a big topic. Like, what *about* friendship?"

That's what we'd figure out together, I thought to myself, but I was too annoyed already to say that.

"Fine," I said, changing the subject. "What about a song that talks about wishing it was summer when it's winter? I wrote a poem about that once, and I like the idea. You know, looking back at a time when you were happier." *Like I'm doing right now,* I added silently to myself.

"Ugh, no," Logan groaned. "That seems sappy."

"Okay," I said between gritted teeth. I moved on to my next idea. And the one after that. And the one after *that.* Logan disliked all of them. Every time Logan said no, I got more upset, but I held it in.

Be professional, I told myself. *Professional musicians don't get mad just because someone disagrees with them. They stay focused on the music.*

TENNEY SHARES THE STAGE

I went through my entire list of ideas (except for Holliday's otter idea), and Logan rejected every single one. When I got to the end, I took a deep breath.

"Do you have any ideas?" I asked Logan.

Logan's expression turned sour, and he shrugged again. Then he thrummed his guitar, sending a few shimmery chords into the room. "I haven't really thought about it yet," he said.

"Really?" I squeaked in disbelief. I couldn't help myself; I was super frustrated. "Zane told us we should come to this session with ideas."

Logan gave me a sharp look. "I haven't had time," he said. "Anyway, I think we should just play our set and see how it goes."

"What do you mean, 'see how it goes'?" I replied tartly. "We're supposed to have ideas to play for Portia on Thursday. In a couple of weeks, Zane's going to want to hear something."

"We'll figure something out at Portia's, okay?" he shot back. "I just don't feel like doing it right now."

My heart was an angry fireball in my chest,

but I refused to let Logan see how mad I was, even though I really wanted to yell at him. *Stay professional,* I reminded myself again.

"Fine," I said at last. *Portia will handle this,* I thought. *I'm sure of it.*

"Fine," Logan said. He hung the guitar back on the wall and got behind his kit.

He nodded, putting up his drumsticks. We started playing "Reach the Sky," not looking at each other. When I closed my eyes, the music sounded fine. As soon as I opened them, though, I felt lonely even though Logan was just a few feet away.

We spent the next hour playing through the rest of our old set, pausing to get Dad when customers came in, replaying parts of songs that we often messed up, and taking water breaks when we needed to. The music calmed me down, and I considered bringing up songwriting again. But I didn't know how Logan would react, so I didn't say anything.

Finally, Dad came in from the stockroom and walked toward the front door. "It's six," he said, turning the OPEN sign to CLOSED.

TENNEY SHARES THE STAGE

Logan hopped off the stage. "I should get going," he said.

I breathed a sigh of relief. I was still disappointed that we hadn't gotten any songwriting done, but at least I didn't have to look at Logan's sour expression anymore today.

We gathered up our stuff and went outside.

"Is your mom picking you up?" Dad asked Logan.

Logan shook his head. "I'm riding my bike."

"Guess I'll see you Thursday," I said to Logan, barely glancing at him.

"Yep," he said, and moved to the bike rack, heading for an orange bike with silver streaks.

I had turned and started toward Dad's truck when I heard Logan say, "Oh no."

I looked back and saw Logan inspecting a flat tire on his bicycle. "Stupid bike," Logan growled, nudging the tire with the toe of his sneaker. "It's always going flat. I'm so sick of it."

"Do you need a ride home?" Dad asked.

Logan shook his head hard while opening his bike lock. "I'll just roll it."

BE PROFESSIONAL

"Are you sure?" Dad asked, his eyes crinkling with concern.

Logan chewed his lip, thinking. "Do you have a bike pump by any chance?" he finally asked.

"Not here," Dad said, "but there's one at the house, and I have patches. We can put your bike in the back of my truck and fix the tire there. It's just a few blocks away."

Logan looked torn, but he finally nodded.

"Great," Dad said. "You can stay for dinner, too."

"Really?" Logan asked, perking up.

"Yeah, really?" I echoed before I could stop myself. My voice sounded sharp, and I immediately felt bad. Logan's face turned bright red.

"I mean, isn't it late notice for Mom?" I said to Dad.

"I'll ask," Dad said, whipping out his phone and typing a text. "You know her, she always makes extra. I'm sure it'll be fine."

"Okay," I said, trying not to sound as uncomfortable as I felt.

"I should probably ask my mom, too," Logan

said, pulling out his cell phone. "I'll text her."

We waited in silence for Mrs. Everett and Mom to reply. Dad had a goofy grin on his face while Logan and I tried to avoid making eye contact. Within moments of each other, Dad's and Logan's phones chimed.

"My mom says it's okay," Logan told us.

"Georgia says no problemo!" Dad said.

Logan looked relieved. For the first time all day, he cracked a smile.

Dad hoisted the bike over his shoulder and started for his truck. He glanced back at me with a curious squint.

"What are you waiting for, Tenney?" he called.

I realized I'd been standing there, gritting my teeth in silent frustration. The last thing I wanted was to spend more time with Logan right now. But at this moment, it didn't seem like I had a choice.

MUD PIE AND MELODIES

Chapter 3

*W*hen we got home, I could hear Aubrey practicing her accordion through the open window of our living room. Her wheezy song wafted over the porch like a breath of old perfume, pretty but slightly flat. She stopped playing when she saw Logan come through the front door with Dad and me.

"Logan!" she shouted. She dropped her accordion on the couch, raced over, and threw her arms around him. He looked surprised, but he hugged her back.

"Where's Mason?" I asked. Mason's my big brother. I thought maybe he could keep Logan company so I wouldn't have to.

"Probably in the garage fixing another broken amp," Dad said.

Logan's face brightened at the mention of amplifiers. Before he could say anything, though, our golden retriever, Waylon, popped up from behind the couch and started licking Logan's hand.

"Whoa!" Logan said, stepping back.

Aubrey giggled. And even though I felt weird that Logan was here, I couldn't help cracking a smile, too.

"That's just Waylon," I said. "Don't worry, he's a lover, not a biter."

Waylon gave a friendly bark like he was agreeing with me, and Logan looked reassured.

"Hey there!" Mom said, poking her head in from the kitchen. "Logan, you hungry? We're having spaghetti and turkey meatballs, broccoli, garlic bread, and mud pie for dessert."

"But you only get dessert if you eat your broccoli," Aubrey told him. "That's a family rule."

"I actually like broccoli," Logan admitted.

"You can have mine!" Aubrey said eagerly.

We all laughed, even Logan. He seemed different to me now than he had during rehearsal. Less wound up somehow.

"I'm so glad you're here!" Aubrey told him, grabbing his hand. "Now you can hear me play my

MUD PIE AND MELODIES

accordion!" She pulled him over to the couch.

Dad smiled and shook his head before heading into the kitchen to help Mom. I inhaled, breathing in the warm, cheesy garlic smell of tonight's dinner. Suddenly, my mouth was watering.

I excused myself to set the table in the kitchen, keeping an eye on Aubrey's private accordion concert for Logan in the living room. I was worried that he would be rude to Aubrey and try to "fix" her playing somehow, the way he sometimes did with me. But he listened politely, even offering her an encouraging smile as she played her newest song.

I placed the last water glass on the table and leaned against the doorway to watch as Aubrey squeezed out the final notes of her song. The accordion was almost too big for her, but she pushed and pulled, notes cascading out in a melody. I could tell she'd been practicing from how smoothly she played. When she finished, Logan and I applauded.

"That was awesome!" he exclaimed.

Aubrey stood up and did a proud little bow, hugging her accordion. "It's hard to work the bellows because my arms are small," Aubrey told him, puffing as she squashed in the shiny red accordion to let out a wheezy chord.

"I'm really impressed," Logan told her. "I could never play the accordion; it's really tough."

Aubrey beamed, and my annoyance at Logan melted a little. *He's being really nice,* I thought. *Maybe he was such a pain at rehearsal because he'd had a bad day at school or something.*

As the night went on, Logan continued to warm up to my family. When Mason came in from working in the garage, Logan asked him about the amplifiers he was fixing up. At dinner, he cleaned his plate and answered all my parents' questions. In the time it took to eat one plate of spaghetti and meatballs, I learned that Logan was born in Pigeon Forge, had a younger brother, and liked bike riding and Indian food. If I'd known that eating was the secret to getting him to open up, I would have brought brownies to every rehearsal.

"I haven't really had much of a chance to talk to you about music, Logan," Mom said as she served him more spaghetti and meatballs. "I know

MUD PIE AND MELODIES

your father's a guitarist, but does your mom play an instrument?"

Logan shook his head. "It's more my dad's thing. He taught me guitar."

"How'd you learn drums?" Dad asked.

Logan shrugged. "On my own. I taught myself by watching videos online."

"Wow," Mason said, impressed. Mason plays drums, too, but he took lessons. "You're even more talented than we realized."

Logan turned bright red and studied his plate. I had to admit, it *was* impressive. Drums aren't easy to learn, but Logan was a skilled player. It made me wonder how well he played guitar. I hadn't heard more than an E chord out of him during our short-lived songwriting session.

"How long have you played guitar?" I asked.

"Since I was four," Logan replied.

"That's how old Tenney was when she insisted that I teach her to play," Dad said, chuckling. "Your parents must be proud."

"Now why haven't we met your dad yet?" Mom asked. "Is he still on tour?"

TENNEY SHARES THE STAGE

"Um, yeah," Logan said, his eyes flicking down to his plate. "I think he's in Japan right now."

Logan's dad had been on tour the whole time I'd known him. For a moment I imagined traveling the world, learning about new cultures and performing on a different stage every night.

"That's so cool," I said.

"I guess," Logan replied, but he didn't look like he thought it was cool. He looked the way Waylon does when we put him in a crate to go to the vet. Logan was acting like his dad being a professional musician was boring or something. *Weird.*

"Hey," Dad said suddenly. "Did I ever tell you guys about when my high school rock band booked our own tour through eastern Tennessee?"

Mason, Aubrey, and I groaned, but Dad ignored us. "It's an epic journey involving a seventy-nine Cadillac, a spontaneously combusting amplifier, and an audience of very upset heavy metal fans," he told Logan.

"You've told this story fifty times," Mason said.

"Because it's a great story!" Dad insisted. "Trust me, the only thing better than touring is

MUD PIE AND MELODIES

being able to talk about it afterward."

"I want to hear what happened," Logan said. He seemed genuinely interested.

We all listened as Dad recounted his crazy adventures playing in town squares and high school gyms. Then Logan asked Dad about what songs he'd performed ... which led to Aubrey asking how "Achy Breaky Heart" goes ... which led to Mom singing it. And pretty soon everyone was singing along, even Logan. By the end of dinner, he had a grin on his face wider than the state of Tennessee. I couldn't remember ever seeing him look happier.

Once the dishes were cleared, Dad headed to the garage to fix Logan's bike. "It'll just take a minute," he said.

Aubrey and Mason were helping with dishes, so Mom waved Logan and me into the living room.

Waylon was sprawled on the rug by a back wall, where our family's musical instrument collection hung. Logan bent down to scratch Waylon's ears, his gaze drifting past Dad's guitars, Mom's Autoharp, and Mason's mandolin to the older antique instruments near the ceiling.

TENNEY SHARES THE STAGE

"Do you guys actually play all these?" he asked.

"The ones hanging up top are too delicate," I said, "but the rest of them get played a lot. We used to jam together as a family every Sunday. We haven't done it in a while 'cause things have been so busy." I sighed. "I really miss it."

Right then an idea popped into my head. "Hey! You should come over sometime and jam with us!" *Wait . . . did I just say that?* I asked myself. This was definitely not how I expected this day to end up.

"Maybe sometime," Logan said. He looked out the window at the darkening sky. "You're pretty lucky, Tenney," he said. "I mean, your life, your family, and being surrounded by all this music? It's amazing."

I nodded, suddenly feeling self-conscious. "Yeah," I said. "I love being able to share my music with my family."

Logan looked down at his shoes. It seemed like he wanted to say something, but he snapped his mouth shut. Another moment of silence passed, and he turned back to the instrument wall.

"What a cool guitar," Logan said, running his hand down a small one with red frets.

MUD PIE AND MELODIES

"That's a *tres* guitar, from Cuba," I said. "It's mostly used for salsa music. See how the strings are set differently?" I pointed out the fret board. "They're set in pairs. You play it more like a rhythm instrument."

"Oh yeah," Logan said, looking closer.

"You can try it if you want," I said.

Logan looked thrilled. He lifted the guitar off its wall hook and strummed it. A rich wave of sound came out, and Logan smiled. "Might be a little too complicated for me," he admitted.

He scanned the instruments again and nodded at a small, scratched-up guitar off to the side. "What about the one at the end?"

"*That* one?" I asked. "It's just my ol' beater." Ever since Dad had given me my new mini Taylor a few months ago, I had put aside my old guitar.

"It looks like the guitar my dad taught me on. Let me try it," Logan said, trading me the *tres* for my beater. He hugged the old guitar close, like he knew it well. He adjusted the tuning and turned toward the window. Outside, the big oak tree I love glowed in the moonlight. With his

eyes fixed on the tree, Logan began picking out
a melody on the guitar. It was light and catchy,
and as I listened, I realized Logan was an excellent guitar player.

"I like that tune," I said. "Where did you hear it?"

Logan stopped playing, as if he'd just remembered I was there.

"I wrote it," he said, ducking his head shyly.
Thank goodness he wasn't looking at me, because
my jaw dropped in surprise.

"Wow," I said. Logan's songs were usually fast-
paced and hard-edged. I'd never heard Logan play
anything so fun and upbeat before. It was very
un-Logan.

"It's not finished yet," Logan said. "I'm still
working on a chorus."

"Well, what you've got so far is great," I said in
a rush. "Why didn't you play it at rehearsal when I
asked if you had any song ideas?"

Logan looked sort of embarrassed. "I don't really
know," he said. "I guess I didn't think you'd like it."

"Are you kidding? It's great!" I said. "We
should work on it together!" The thought burst out

of me before I'd even decided to say it.

"You mean write it together?" said Logan, looking surprised.

"Yes," I said.

He squinted at me for a moment, as if he were trying to decide whether to tell me a secret.

"Okay," he said at last.

"Great!" I said. Suddenly, we were beaming at each other.

"Logan! Tenney!" Dad called to us through the window screen.

We hung up the guitars and went outside.

"The tire needed a patch," Dad explained to Logan, showing him the bike's front wheel. "It's fixed now, but the rubber's wearing out all over. You should get a new tire when you can."

"Um, sure," Logan said. He stepped forward to take the bike, but Dad rolled it back.

"It's getting dark," Dad said. "We'll drive you home."

Logan shook his head. "That's okay. I have a helmet and reflective gear, and it's not far—"

"We're driving you home," Dad repeated, and

the tone in his voice said it was a done deal.

A few minutes later, I was buckled in between Dad and Logan in the front seat of Dad's truck. I looked out the window as we drove into Logan's neighborhood. Night had fallen, and there weren't too many streetlights, so it was hard to see. The houses were smaller than the ones on our block, and the trees were taller. Although we were only a few miles from our house in the city, it felt like we were out in the country.

We turned down Logan's street. "You can just pull over there," he said, gesturing to a small white house in the middle of the block. Dad slowed the truck to a stop, and Logan hopped out.

"Thanks for having me over for dinner," Logan said to me, as Dad got his bike off the truck bed. "It was really fun."

"I know," I agreed, feeling a twinge of surprise. "I'm excited to work on our song."

"Me, too," Logan said shyly. "See you at Portia's on Thursday." With that, he took his bike by the handlebars and wheeled his way up the long dirt driveway into shadows.

OUT OF TUNE

Chapter 4

*W*hen we got home, I went up to my room to think. My bedroom isn't small, but I share it with Aubrey, so it never quite feels big enough. I crossed the room, walking past the glittery mound of shoes, clothes, and accordion stuff on Aubrey's side, and flopped onto my bed. Ever since we'd dropped Logan off at his house, I couldn't stop wondering whether he and I were *real* friends. I still wasn't totally sure.

Logan confused me. I'd always respected his musical skills, but when we first met, I couldn't stand his rude arrogance, and I had trouble keeping track of his moods. This afternoon, he was grouchy during most of rehearsal, but he seemed like a completely different person when he came over for dinner. He was patient with Aubrey and polite to my parents and Mason. What's more, the melody Logan had played for me after dinner was sweet in a way that didn't seem like the Logan I knew. I didn't know what to make of it.

I sat up and pulled my guitar into my lap. My fingers settled on the strings, and I started picking out Logan's melody. I don't always remember every piece of music I hear, but his tune had stuck in my head. It was light and catchy, but it had a yearning feeling, too. Like an unfinished wish.

Logan had been right when he said it wasn't done yet. He'd come up with a bright, pretty melody for the verses, but that was it. For a song to be complete, it needed a chorus, a bridge, an ending, and a sense of "going somewhere," as Portia always said.

I sighed. We were meeting Portia for a songwriting session on Thursday after school. I didn't want to show up with half an idea. *Logan agreed we should write the song together,* I told myself. *If I come up with a few ideas now, it'll make it easier for us to co-write with Portia. It might even be fun.*

I played through the melody again. It started

OUT OF TUNE

out strong, but got a little muddled at the end of the verse. I started over, simplifying the last couple of measures to complete the phrase. Then I found a natural chorus melody that complemented the song's main theme.

By the time Aubrey came in to put on her pajamas, I had nailed down everything except the bridge and the outro, but I felt like the song was one step closer to being done. I realized I was actually looking forward to hearing what Logan thought of my changes. *Maybe collaborating with Logan won't be so bad after all,* I thought.

When school got out on Thursday, I stopped by Dad's store to grab my guitar and headed to Portia's cottage.

Portia greeted me at the front door, her cheeks as pink as blooming roses. She wore an embroidered blouse, and her steel-gray hair was coiled in a braid around her head. Silver drop earrings twinkled on her ears. They jingled as she tilted her head at me, making her own unique percussion.

"Welcome!" she said. As she led me inside, I noticed she was holding a strange contraption: a metal loop with two thick black plastic handles.

"What kind of instrument is that?" I asked, lugging my guitar case into the comfy living room.

"This?" Portia said, holding up the metal thingy with a laugh. "It's not an instrument. It's a handgrip. I have to squeeze it thirty times a day as part of my physical therapy."

"Oh, right," I said. Over a year and a half ago, Portia had a stroke that had paralyzed her chord hand. She was mostly recovered now, but she still did exercises to restore the strength she lost.

"Does it hurt your hand to use it?" I wondered.

"Not anymore," Portia said, squeezing the grip a few times fast. "When I started, it was tougher, but these days doing it makes me feel like Wonder Woman." She put up her arm in a muscle-woman pose, and I laughed.

"To tell you the truth, though, nothing's helped me more than playing my guitar," Portia continued. "The best way to heal from anything is to do what you love. For me, that's playing music."

I nodded enthusiastically. She was right; playing music always made me feel better. I loved working with Portia, because every time I saw her, she taught me something about music, and even more about myself.

I had arrived early for our songwriting session, so Portia poured me some sweet tea and we chatted while I got out my guitar. To warm up, I played one of Portia's songs, "April Springs." Portia gave me pointers on my finger placement on the frets and advised me to tense up the wrist of my strumming hand to get a richer sound. I couldn't help but smile. "April Springs" has always been one of my favorites, even before I knew Portia had written it. The song was a big hit years ago, when Portia was performing under the stage name Patty Burns. Playing it now, I remembered how shocked and thrilled I was when I first realized Portia had written a song that I loved. And now here I was, in Portia's living room, getting advice from the songwriter herself.

TENNEY SHARES THE STAGE

It was so much fun, I almost forgot why I was there . . . until Portia frowned at the clock on her mantel.

"Where *is* Logan?" she asked.

I looked at the time. Logan was more than fifteen minutes late.

"I'm not sure," I admitted. "He said he'd be here when I saw him on Tuesday."

Portia's eyes sharpened, but she just nodded and crossed her arms over her chest.

Ten minutes later, we heard a soft *whoosh* in Portia's driveway. I peered outside. Logan was locking his orange-and-silver bike to the chain-link fence. His face looked like a storm cloud about to burst.

"How nice of you to join us, Mr. Everett," Portia said sharply as Logan slipped through the door and into the sitting room.

Logan didn't apologize. "I need to borrow a guitar," he said, his voice gruff.

Portia raised her eyebrows. "Over there," she said finally, waving at some guitars clustered on stands in a corner. Logan stalked over and picked up the nearest one. He didn't say a word as he plunked down next to me on the sofa.

"So I know you two have started writing together," Portia said. "Why don't you play me what you've been working on?"

I glanced at Logan, but he sat there like a bump on a log. So I told Portia about Logan's tune.

"I've been trying out different ways to transition the verse melody into the new chorus that I added," I started, peering back to Logan.

I thought he'd be pleased. Instead, suspicion ignited in his eyes.

"What does that mean? You just went off and rewrote it without me?" he said sharply.

"No, I brainstormed ideas," I corrected him, trying to keep cool. "That's it."

Logan scowled, but I didn't flinch. *You agreed to this,* I told him with my eyes. *I'm not backing down.*

"Whatever," he mumbled at last. "I'll play *my* melody for Portia first."

"Fine," I said. I swallowed my frustration and laid my guitar on my knees.

Logan started playing, attacking his guitar like

he was mad at it. Suddenly, his fun, bouncy song sounded loud and grating. I couldn't help but wince.

"Slow down," Portia told Logan over the music. He did, which made it sound even worse. When he was done, Portia turned to me.

"So, Tenney, what were your ideas?" she said.

"Well, I made the end of the phrase a little simpler, for a start," I said. I played Logan's melody from the top, then went right into the chorus I'd come up with. Before I'd even finished, Logan was shaking his head.

"It's too cute," he said.

"What does *that* mean?" I said, annoyance streaking through me.

"It means I don't like it," Logan replied bluntly.

"Do you have a better idea?" I shot back.

Logan opened his mouth, then closed it again, clearly struggling. I smirked, satisfied that my point had been made.

"Both of y'all, take it down a notch," Portia said gently. "Instead of getting riled up, let's try brainstorming together. Logan, how about you try to riff off of Tenney's chorus idea."

"Okay," Logan said. He attacked his guitar strings, playing what sounded like a whole lot of angry noise.

"Are you kidding?" I blurted, even before he'd finished.

Logan clapped a hand over his strings, silencing the guitar. "You don't like it?" he asked.

"Of course I don't like it! It's awful!" I said, my voice flaring into a yell. I turned to Portia. "He's not even trying to collaborate!"

"Neither are you!" Logan threw back at me.

I was hoping Portia would take my side, but she kept silent. Right as I was getting uncomfortable, she stood up. "I'm going to go make myself some tea."

"Now?" I said.

"Yup!" said Portia. "I'll be gone for a while."

"Why?" Logan said, sounding uncertain.

"Because you two need to work this out on your own," Portia said.

"W-what?!" I stuttered. Panic rang inside me like a fire alarm. Zane had promised that Portia would help Logan and me work through our problems. And now she was abandoning us?

Portia crossed her arms, regarding us. "I want you both to take a deep breath and answer one question: Why are you arguing?"

"Because we have different opinions," Logan said.

"No, because we have different personalities," I corrected him.

"You're both wrong," Portia said matter-of-factly. "You're arguing because you're not dealing with your differences respectfully. In order to collaborate, you need to be able to disagree without making it personal. If you can't handle that, you probably shouldn't be working together."

"Exactly," I muttered.

Portia zeroed in on me, her eyes as sharp as pins. "Except maybe as a team, you make each other better," she said. Her words hung in the air for a few moments.

"I've been co-writing for thirty years, and I've learned the hard way that two people can't write a song without trust," she continued. "You need to trust yourself to be honest and vulnerable. And you need to trust the process. You can get over disagreements if you keep in mind that every song goes through rough patches. The most important thing, though, is to trust your writing partner." She looked me in the eye. "It doesn't matter if it's hard—you have to be honest, say what you feel, and trust that your partner's going to listen with open ears." Then she turned to Logan. "And you need to trust that Tenney wants what's best for the song, just like you do. Because at the end of the day, you have to do what's best for your music," she finished, her eyes cool and sharp. "So? Do you trust each other?"

I bit my lip. Logan shrugged. Neither of us said anything.

"Okay then, that's what you need to work on first," Portia said. "Because if you can't trust each other, well, then, I don't know if I can help you."

She moved to the door and looked back at us.

"You have half an hour. After that, let's hear what you come up with together." And with that, she disappeared into the kitchen.

Logan and I sat there, not looking at each other.

"All of this is your fault," I whispered. "If you

hadn't been late and picked a fight, she wouldn't have gotten mad."

"You're the one who went off and tried writing my own song without me!" he hissed.

I wanted to snap at him, but I bit my tongue. I didn't want to make things worse.

We sat for a long while, holding our guitars. In the silence, it felt like the sea was quieting after a storm.

"I'm sorry your feelings got hurt," I said. "I was just trying to get us started."

Logan studied his feet. "It's okay," he mumbled after a moment. "I should have asked you not to work on it without me. Sorry I blew up."

"Okay," I said.

We sat in silence for a while longer, not sure what to say next.

At last, I spoke. "I know this is tough, but we have to try at least. Right?"

Logan nodded. He resettled Portia's guitar on his knees. His fingers drifted across the fret board, picking out a few thoughtful notes.

"I actually liked *part* of your chorus," he said,

talking over the music, "but I feel like something doesn't work about how it comes out of the verse melody." He played the section again. He was right: Something didn't match up.

"I hear that," I said, playing the transition again. "What about something like this?" I replayed it, this time adding a few notes to the measure.

Logan cocked his head. "That's better . . . but what if we try this?" he said, changing a couple of notes. All of a sudden, the chorus felt brighter. I liked it immediately.

"Yes!" I said.

Logan looked encouraged—and a little vulnerable. "Um, I've also been thinking that the bridge needs to be just a short instrumental break, so we can get back to the chorus at the end," he said.

"I hear you," I agreed. I drummed my fingers on my guitar's neck. "What about adding a few wrap-up lines to the second chorus? Something like this?" I played a variation on the chorus melody that built to a bigger climax.

"I like it!" Logan said. He played it back to me, tightening some notes.

TENNEY SHARES THE STAGE

It sounded better, and we both grinned.

"Let's play it together from the top," I said.

And so we did, both of us nodding to the beat. When we finished, Logan had an idea. Then I got an idea from his idea. We didn't talk much. We mostly just said, "How about this?" and played bits of the song back and forth, working on different moments that could be better. I lost track of time. It felt like five minutes had passed when Portia popped her head in.

"You ready?" she said.

"We're still working," I said, a little breathless. Portia cracked a smile.

"You've been at it for an hour," she said. Logan and I looked at each other, surprised.

"I guess we can play what we have so far," Logan said.

"It's still rough, though," I added.

"Rough is a start," Portia said, settling into her armchair. "Let me hear it."

"I'll play guitar, you hum the melody, okay?" Logan said, and I nodded.

We started slowly. There were a few bumps,

but after a verse, we slipped into a rhythm. By the time we finished, Portia was smiling.

"Now that sounds like the start of a *real* song!" she said. "How was it working together?"

"Hard at first," Logan admitted, "but it got easier."

"Yeah," I agreed.

"Well, you've got a good, solid song structure there; just keep refining it," said Portia. "Let's meet again on Sunday. I'll invite Zane to come over and hear it."

Worry rippled through me. What if Zane heard our rough version and didn't think it was good enough for our EP? "It's too early to play it for Zane," I said. "We need to work out lyrics first."

I turned to Logan, hoping he'd back me up, but he was already walking across the room, Portia's guitar in hand.

"What are you doing?" I asked.

"I have to go," he said, settling the guitar back on its stand.

"Now? But what about the lyrics?" I protested.

Logan gave me a little smile. "We don't have to

finish the song today, Tenney."

Before I could respond, he hiked his backpack onto his shoulder and hustled toward the door. "See you on Sunday, Portia," he called back, letting the screen door slam behind him.

Portia shook her head. "Now he was itchier to get out of here than a rabbit in a foxhole," she noted.

She turned to me and put her hands on my shoulders. "I'm proud of the progress you made today, Tenney."

"Thanks," I said. As we hugged, I peered around her shoulder to see if I could catch Logan before he left. Sure enough, he was still fiddling with his bike lock.

I quickly packed up my guitar and said good-bye to Portia.

Logan was halfway down the street when I got outside.

"Logan!" I called to him.

He screeched to a stop and looked over his shoulder. "What?" he said, sounding annoyed.

I squared my shoulders. "I really think we

should add an extra songwriting session to our rehearsal schedule so that we have something more finished to play for Zane on Sunday."

"I don't have time for another session," he said with a shrug. "You write the lyrics, Tenney. You're better with words than me, anyway."

Huh? First he was mad at me for working on his song without him. Now he was ordering me to work on my own again after we had just finished a great session together! My cheeks got hot. I wasn't sure if I should be flattered that Logan trusted me with writing the lyrics or annoyed that he was leaving the work to me.

Besides, what if I wrote the lyrics and Logan hated them? We had been able to work through our differences this time, but who knew how he would act at our next rehearsal. Logan's mood swings made me nervous. I loved the way we sounded when we played together, but I knew now that this wasn't enough to build a successful career in music as a duo. Deep down, I had to admit, I wasn't sure if my musical partnership with Logan was strong enough to last.

SING YOUR MIND

Chapter 5

"**T**enney, those dishes are clean." Mom's voice broke into my thoughts, gentle but persistent. I looked down at the open dishwasher, where I was about to put a sticky, crumb-splattered bowl. It was full of gleaming silverware and plates.

"Oh, right," I said, embarrassment heating my cheeks.

I dunked the dirty bowl back in the sink, where the rest of the dishes from dinner were soaking. I wiped my hands on a dish towel and started putting away the clean dishes. Mom leaned against the kitchen counter next to me, watching.

"Are you okay?" she said. "You were a million miles away at dinner."

"I was just thinking about a song," I said, avoiding her gaze.

SING YOUR MIND

It wasn't really a lie. I *had* been thinking about the song Logan and I had worked on this afternoon, but I'd been thinking even more about Logan's strange, moody behavior. I wanted to talk to Mom about it, but I hesitated. Mom really liked Logan, and I didn't want to hear from yet another well-intentioned adult that I needed to try a little harder to get along with him. *You signed a contract to be musical partners,* I could hear her say. *That means you've got to learn how to work with him, no matter what.*

"Really, I'm fine," I told Mom, forcing a smile. "You know how I get when I've got a song in my brain. I just have to get it out."

I think Mom could sense I didn't want to be pushed, because she gave my shoulder a squeeze. "Okay," she said, easing past me to the living room. "You know where I am if you want to talk about it."

Once I was alone, my heart felt heavy. Maybe there was something to the line I had given Mom, and I just needed to get out my emotions. I thought of what Portia had said earlier this afternoon: *The best way to heal from anything is to do what you love.*

I'll work on the song lyrics, I thought, carrying
a stack of plates over to a cabinet. *Logan told me to
write them on my own. That's exactly what I'll do.*

I looked through the glass door that opened
out to our backyard. The grass shimmered with
chilly evening dew. *So much for writing outside,*
I thought. I went into the living room. Mason
was showing Mom something on his phone.
Waylon was asleep on the couch beside Dad,
who was coaching Aubrey through a new song
on her accordion. They barely noticed as I passed
through on my way upstairs.

I closed my bedroom door behind me and
grabbed my guitar from its stand at the end of my
bed. Then I slipped its wide leather strap over my
head, shifting the instrument into place on my
body. I walked the room, testing each guitar string
to make sure it was in tune.

My eyes drifted to a small window next
to Aubrey's desk that overlooked our backyard.
Through it, I saw a patch of blue-black night sky
and a cloud of silvery oak leaves and branches.

SING YOUR MIND

I didn't look out at this view very often, I realized. It was a new perspective. I liked it.

I settled my fingers on my guitar strings and started playing the tune Logan and I had worked on this afternoon. The melody was quick and fun, and as it flowed through me, I felt proud of what Logan and I had created together.

But uneasy moments kept flashing through my head. The way Logan had rushed out of our meeting with Portia. The tone in his voice when he'd called my ideas "cute." His shrug when he told me I should write the lyrics. He hadn't even asked if I wanted to write them; he'd just said it like he had decided for both of us.

Of course, I *did* want to write the lyrics, I admitted to myself, but that wasn't the point. Deep down, it still didn't feel like Logan and I were a team.

I stopped playing, frustration and uncertainty storming inside me. I realized that I needed to let Logan know how he made me feel.

Setting my guitar on the floor, I grabbed my songwriting journal from my nightstand. I curled

up on my bed, grabbed a pen, and flipped the
journal open to the first blank page, near the back.
I started listing everything I'd been too polite to say
to Logan since we'd started playing together:

You don't listen to me.
You're rude.
You change your mind all the time.
You're unpredictable.
You're hot and cold.
You shut me out.
I can't tell what you're thinking.
I can't trust you.

I paused. After all we'd accomplished today,
I knew it was harsh to say I still didn't trust Logan,
but at this moment, it was truly what I felt.

I kept writing, emotions flooding through my
pen. I hadn't fully understood how much I wanted
to say to Logan, but before I knew it, I'd scrawled
down two full pages of thoughts and feelings.
When my hand started to cramp, I put down my
pen and stretched my fingers, looking at what

SING YOUR MIND

I'd written. It didn't all make sense, but putting it down on the page had helped me feel better.

Not only that, I could see what I wanted our song to say.

I started on the lyrics. First, I tore out my two sheets of brainstorm notes. Then I used scissors to cut out each idea, and started arranging each piece of paper on the floor. *This idea could be in the first verse,* I thought, placing a piece of paper to my left. *This one is better for the chorus,* I decided, placing another slip in front of me. Piece by piece, thought by thought, I could *feel* in the pit of my stomach which lines worked best together.

I opened to the next clean page in my journal, and I wrote down the number of beats in each line of our song's verse pattern. Then I got to work stringing my thoughts into a verse that made sense. When I was done with the first verse, I did the same with the second.

I wanted the chorus to tell Logan that I was sick of him being moody and angry, but also that I wished we could understand each other. I figured out something with the right rhythm quickly, then

laid out the third and fourth verses. Once I had
a rough sense of how the song would unfold,
I started rewriting. I flip-flopped phrases and
changed words, sharpening my thoughts. I went
through the lyrics over and over, making sure
each line flowed into the next, rhyming tightly and
matching the number of beats needed. My guitar
sat across the room, but I didn't need it—the melody
played in my head as loudly as if I had speakers
inside my ears.

Finally, I took a break. I took a few deep breaths
and squeezed my eyes closed. Then I opened them
and read all my lyrics. To my surprise, I didn't want
to throw my journal against a wall or rip up what I'd
written. In fact, I didn't really want to change much
of anything. That's how I knew I was done, at least
for now.

Okay, I thought. Hugging my journal, I moved
to my desk and sat down in front of my laptop.

I typed up the song lyrics, every word ringing
out clearly in my head. At the top of the page I wrote
"The Nerve." I saved the document and then
opened my e-mail. I didn't want to wait until our

next rehearsal to share my lyrics with Logan. *If he wants lyrics,* I thought, *I'll give him lyrics.*

I started a new e-mail, entered Logan's address, and typed "New Song Lyrics" in the subject line. Then I pasted the lyrics into the body of the e-mail. As I scanned the words I'd written one last time, I felt a pang of guilt. Would Logan be hurt by what I wrote? I wasn't sure. All I knew was that I was proud that my lyrics told Logan exactly how I was feeling in a way that I never could have told him face-to-face.

If Logan and I are going to trust each other, I thought, *I have to be honest with him.*

Before I could lose my courage, I clicked SEND.

It wasn't until the e-mail *whoosh* sounded that I realized I'd been holding my breath. I let out a sigh. I had no idea how Logan would react to the lyrics. I just hoped he would get the message that no matter how rude he acted, I wasn't going to let it stop me from making music.

TENNEY SHARES THE STAGE

I was getting into my pajamas when my phone shuddered with a cymbal crash from my nightstand. I'd picked that sound for Logan's texts, partly because he played drums but also because, like percussion, Logan sometimes gave me a headache.

Curiosity shivered through me. I checked my phone. On the screen was Logan's text:

Got the lyrics. Good job. Let's meet at your dad's store tomorrow after school and keep working on it.

"Okay," I texted back, but I was a little surprised. *Good job?* Is that really all Logan had to say about what I'd written? Usually, he was so critical. Plus, I'd basically used the song to list all the things about him that annoyed me. Could it be possible that he hadn't noticed that? I wasn't sure, but I didn't feel like discussing it through texts. I was going to have to wait until tomorrow to find out exactly how Logan felt about my lyrics.

FACING THE MUSIC

Chapter 6

*W*hen Mason and I arrived at Dad's music store the next day, Logan was locking his bike to the rack nearby.

"Hey," he said with a cheery wave.

I waited for him to say something about the lyrics I'd sent, but instead he turned to Mason and started talking about amplifiers.

Dad poked his head around a rack of guitar strings by the door as we walked in. "Well, if it isn't Double Trouble!" he said. "What do you think of that band name, Tenney?"

"Daaad . . ." I said, turning pink.

Dad waggled his eyebrows. "You don't like it? How about the Dangerous Duo? Or Partners in Crime? Twice as Nice? I could go on for days . . ."

"Please don't," Mason said playfully before

heading to the storeroom to do his homework.

Dad chuckled. He turned back to me and Logan. "So! Where are you two thinking you want to work?"

"Um, maybe not the stage," I said, glancing over at the low platform where we rehearsed last time. "Can we use the listening room?"

"Sure thing," Dad said. I nodded, relieved. Working on this song with Logan was going to be tricky enough with the new lyrics I'd written. I didn't want to do it in front of Dad and Mason.

Logan chose a guitar from the instrument wall and we made our way through the store to the listening room in back. It's a small room, but it has high ceilings and the acoustics are good. Logan and I squeezed inside. Without saying a word, we both began warming up, sending quick, silvery notes through the air.

"We should start with the new song," I said over the sound.

Logan nodded, strumming a dramatic riff. "I revised your lyrics," he said nonchalantly.

I stopped playing my scales, caught off guard. "Oh?"

FACING THE MUSIC

"Well, not every line," Logan corrected. He let out another ripple of notes with a flourish. "Just the second verse. And I changed a couple of lines in the third verse."

I nodded, but I felt a twinge of worry. We were co-writing the song, so I couldn't complain about Logan adding his own lyrics. Still, I was nervous about what he'd added.

I think Logan could tell. "Let's play the song through together," he suggested. "Then you can hear it. You sing the first verse, and I'll sing the second."

I nodded. We counted off and launched into the song's intro. The shimmery sound of Logan's guitar melted into the deeper, woodsier twang of mine as we overlapped. Then I started singing.

I don't like the way you shrug
like you've got nothin' else to say
And I don't like the way you always
want to do it your way

I watched Logan carefully as I sang. He didn't *seem* upset. I continued the second half of the verse.

TENNEY SHARES THE STAGE

You turn around and do
exactly what I ask you not to
And I can feel you criticizing
every move I make

And it seems like I'm the only one
that's trying here

Logan still didn't seem upset, even during
the part when I said he wasn't really trying. I felt
relieved and confused all at once. As we moved
into the second verse, I loosened my pick hand and
strummed softly, letting Logan take the lead as we
reached his verse.

I don't like the way you think
that you know all there is to know
I don't like the way you think
you're better all on your own

I gasped, immediately recognizing what
Logan had done: He had written lyrics about *me*.
I gave him a pointed stare, but if he noticed, he

didn't show it. He just kept singing.

> *I turn around and do*
> *exactly what I need to do*
> *'Cause you're always moving*
> *just a little bit too slow*
>
> *And it seems like I'm the only one*
> *that's trying here*

Yep, Logan's lyrics were clearly about all the things I did that annoyed him. Hurt feelings formed a lump in my throat. My face got hot, but I tried to ignore it, focusing on my guitar. My pride felt bruised, but the songwriting part of my brain had to admit that Logan's verse was clever and honest. Logan had revised my lyrics and added *his* voice to the song. *Now we both got to say how we feel,* I thought.

I joined him on the chorus, my voice growing stronger as he added his harmony.

> *You've got the nerve*
> *to act like I'm the one*

TENNEY SHARES THE STAGE

who makes this hard
It makes me hurt
to think that we might
mess this up
And I'm done letting you
I can't get through to you

There were two measures at the end of the chorus that we'd added as an instrumental transition—but to my surprise, Logan sang two new lines instead.

Let's meet this head-on
I'll let you get on my last nerve

A slow smile curled onto my face. Logan stopped playing, and so did I.

"What do you think?" he said, and leaned forward, his eyes flickering with something like nervousness.

"It's really good," I replied honestly. "I can't believe you came up with such a great verse!" The moment the words came out, I realized how rude I sounded. "I'm sorry, that came out all wrong," I said.

"It's okay. I knew what you meant," Logan said carefully. "When I first heard your lyrics, I was sort of annoyed. But they also inspired me. I just had to make sure I got my point of view in there, too."

"Oh, you *did*!" I joked. We both laughed.

"What's important is that we're both being honest," I said.

"Right," Logan agreed, his smile fading. He stared down at his guitar uncomfortably. "Listen, I know I've been in kind of a bad mood lately," he said, looking up at me. "I'm sorry. I have a lot of stuff going on."

"Okay," I said, surprised. It sounded like he was trying to open up. I was about to ask him what kind of "stuff" he was talking about, but then I thought maybe he didn't want to talk about it. So I stayed quiet and waited for Logan to speak again.

He twisted his guitar pegs, and for a moment, he looked sort of upset. "I just have a lot on my plate with my family right now," he said finally.

"Like what?" I ventured, but Logan shook his head, hard.

"It's not important," he said, an edge creeping into his voice. He paused and took a deep breath. "My mom just needs me to take care of my little brother, Jude, more often lately. Like, every day."

"Okay," I said, but concern was rising up inside me. "Does that mean you can't rehearse as much?"

"No, it's fine. I can handle it," he said. He leaned forward, his eyes worried. "Do me a favor?" he asked. "Don't mention this to Zane or Portia. I want them to be focused on my music, not worried about whether I'm committed to our band."

"Um . . ." I said uncertainly. Logan's request made me uncomfortable. I didn't like the idea of keeping secrets from Zane and Portia. And if Logan *couldn't* handle it, what would that mean for the future of Tenney & Logan?

"Don't worry," Logan said as if he were reading my mind. "Music is the best thing in my life, and I won't let anything keep me from playing. I can handle it, just . . . promise me you won't tell Zane and Portia."

I opened my mouth, but I didn't know what

to say. I wanted him to be able to trust me—no, I wanted us to be able to trust each other. So I pushed aside my worry and said, "I promise I won't say anything."

"Thanks," Logan replied, sounding relieved. "So, um, should we take it again from the top?"

I nodded, and we started over. When we got to the bridge, Logan riffed on the melody a bit, his fingers flying up and down his frets. I couldn't help but be impressed. *He's just as good at guitar as he is on drums,* I thought. It gave me an idea.

"When we perform this for Zane, maybe we should both play guitar and sing," I suggested. "You know, keep alternating who sings each verse, like we're doing. We could even go back and forth on a third verse."

"That would be cool," Logan said. "We could use an electronic drumbeat for percussion."

"Exactly," I agreed. And then I got the best idea of my life.

"Hey!" I said. "What if we rewrote the lyrics in the last chorus to be about the things that *work* when we play music together?"

Excitement flashed in Logan's eyes. "That's an awesome idea!" he said.

We both started talking at once. I grabbed my songwriting journal and started writing down our ideas as they came to us. Sometimes we interrupted and talked over each other—at one point I had to yell over Logan so he'd hear me—but I never felt hurt or angry, just excited. Between writing down ideas for new lyrics, a thought flashed through my brain: *We're really working together. We're a team.*

It took a good while, but Logan and I finally worked out a new third verse and final chorus that we liked. We sang it together, wailing in harmony. Then we ran through the whole song over and over, working out the kinks. By the end of our fourth time through, Logan's whole face was a smile.

"That was great!" he said.

"I know!" I replied. My cheeks ached from grinning. I couldn't remember the last time I'd had so much fun working on a song.

Logan's phone beeped, and he checked it. I looked at the clock over his head. It was five thirty.

FACING THE MUSIC

We'd been working for over two hours. Time had raced by.

"Sorry, Tenney, but I've gotta go," he said, looking disappointed.

"That's okay," I said. "I think we're done for the day anyway."

We grabbed our instruments and left the listening room. When we reached the front of the store, we saw that Dad was talking to Ellie Cale, Zane's niece. Ellie works for Zane as a talent scout at Mockingbird Records. We had met when she overheard me playing one of my songs at Dad's store and invited me to play at a showcase at the Bluebird Cafe.

Spotting me and Logan, she smiled warmly. "Hey, you two," she said.

"Ellie just came by with some news," Dad said.

"Yes! I was in the neighborhood, and Zane asked me to stop by to see if you guys were here," Ellie said. "He wanted you to know that you've been requested for a very cool gig coming up at Riff's."

"No way!" Logan said. Riff's was a private club

downtown where a lot of big-deal musicians hung out after they played other shows.

"Yep," Ellie said. "And that's not even the best part. You'd be opening for Belle Starr."

My heart skipped at least two beats. "Are you serious?" I squeaked in excitement. Belle Starr's hit songs were all over the radio. Last month, I'd met her in person when Logan and I played at her mansion for the City Music Festival. Still, even the suggestion that a star like her would want us to open for her seemed unreal.

But Ellie looked totally serious. "Belle's taking a break from her world tour and returning to Nashville in a couple of weeks," Ellie said. "While she's home, she wants to do a private show at Riff's, just for family and friends, to try out some new material. Her label called and said she specifically requested you guys as her opening act."

"Wow," Dad said. "Guess she liked what she heard when you performed last month."

Logan and I nodded, dazed.

"This is a huge opportunity, obviously," said Ellie. "Y'all need to get ready for it. Uncle Zane's

FACING THE MUSIC

going to talk about what this all means when he
joins your songwriting session at Portia's house
on Sunday."

I leaned against the wall, my head spinning.
Belle Starr wants us to open for her! Playing at her
house for the City Music Festival had been cool,
but if Logan and I got to open for a star like Belle,
there was no question that Nashville's entire music
community would know who we were by the time
it was over.

Dad started peppering Ellie with questions
about the gig.

Logan leaned over and whispered to me,
"This is all super cool, but I really have to go,
Tenney." Before I could say anything, he'd put
on his backpack and was heading toward the door.

"I'll be right back," I told Dad and Ellie, and
I hustled to the front door.

"Wait! Logan!" I said, ducking out of the shop
and racing after him.

He looked up from unlocking his bike. "Yeah?"
Logan said.

My cheeks turned bright red. Suddenly, I felt

melodramatic for running after him, but there was something I needed to say.

"Portia was right," I blurted out awkwardly. "We do make each other better."

"I agree," Logan said, rolling his bike out of the rack. "We're a good team."

"I can't wait to play our song for Zane and Portia," I said.

"Me, too," he said, flashing a grin. "See you on Sunday, partner."

WHERE
ARE YOU?

Chapter 7

*T*he next day, the song Logan and I had written was stuck on repeat in my brain. I found myself humming it during my morning shower, in the middle of my math homework, and as I rode my bike to Jaya's house for our Saturday-night sleepover. That happens whenever I fall in love with a song, but the fact that Logan and I had worked so hard on this one made me love it even more.

When I told Jaya and Holliday about our chance to open for Belle Starr, they squealed so loudly that Jaya's mom came upstairs and asked if everything was all right. We said yes, and after she walked off, Jaya whispered to me, "I'm so proud of you!"

I couldn't stop smiling, and inside my head the song I'd written with Logan grew louder. I heard both our voices singing. It made me feel like we were a real band, and I couldn't wait to play it for Zane tomorrow.

Mom picked me up the next morning before Jaya and Holliday had even finished their breakfasts. "Good luck," they told me, mouths full of pancake.

I knew Zane would be there promptly at ten o'clock, so Mom dropped me off a little early to give me time to warm up. I hustled up to the front door of Portia's lavender cottage with my guitar case.

Portia opened the door just after my knock. "Hey there," she said, sweeping loose strands of silver hair off her face. "You ready to play some music?"

I nodded. As I followed her inside, excitement about playing the song again put a spring in my step.

"Zane and Logan aren't here yet," Portia said as we entered the sitting room. "So you can just relax."

I set my case down by the sofa and sat. While Portia got me some water, I took out my guitar and started tuning it, looking out the window at the overgrown front yard. I expected to see Logan roll up on his orange-and-silver bike any moment, sandy hair matted under his helmet. But there was no sign of him.

WHERE ARE YOU?

He didn't show up when I was tuning, or playing scales, or running through the song on my own for practice. He didn't show up when Zane arrived, or while Zane and Portia chitchatted, or when I tried to check the time on my phone without looking too obvious about it.

"Where *is* that boy?" Portia said, when we'd been waiting fifteen minutes. She pressed her lips into a disapproving line.

"Let's give him a call," Zane said. He slid out his phone and tried Logan's cell, but there was no answer. No one picked up when he called Logan's house, either.

"I hope everything's okay," I said, frowning. "Maybe there's some emergency."

"Let's hope not," Zane said.

"Tenney, do you want to play the new song on your own?" Portia asked.

I shook my head. "It's a duet," I said. I needed Logan to sing with me for the song to make sense. But even more than that, I was proud of what Logan and I had written together—it wouldn't feel right to play it on my own.

Another twenty minutes passed. Zane still got no answer from Logan's cell and home numbers. And Logan never responded to the *where are you?!!!?!?!?* text that I sent.

"He was late to our last writing session, too," Portia murmured to Zane, her forehead creased with concern.

Zane frowned. "That's not good," he said.

"He wasn't late to our rehearsals at Dad's store," I chimed in, suddenly feeling protective of Logan.

"I'm glad to hear that, but when it comes to your songwriting sessions, Logan needs to act like a professional *all* the time," Zane said sternly.

"Tenney, do you have any idea where he might be?" Portia asked.

I hesitated, remembering what Logan had said about having to babysit his brother more. Part of me wanted to tell Zane and Portia what Logan had told me ... but he'd made me promise not to mention it.

If I tell them, he'll never trust me again, I thought.

Instead, I told Zane and Portia that Logan and I had worked through our song and we both liked it. "Logan was really proud of what we did. He said he couldn't wait to share it with you."

The more I tried to defend him, the more confused I became about Logan's absence. *We were really starting to click musically,* I thought. *I can't believe he would flake out on rehearsal.*

Eventually, Zane told me to go home. I packed up my guitar and went to the front door. When I looked back and saw the grim looks on Portia's and Zane's faces, though, I had to say something.

"I don't think Logan would miss rehearsal on purpose," I said.

"Okay," Zane said.

I opened my mouth, but couldn't find the words to express what I was thinking. I was surprised by how passionately I wanted to defend Logan. A few weeks ago, I would have been happy to never see the kid again. But after writing our song together, I finally felt like Logan and I were on the same team.

I left Portia's and started walking over to Dad's music store, my stomach twisted with worry. When I entered the shop, Dad was behind the cash register and Mason was organizing packs of guitar strings.

"You're back early, honey," Dad said, surprise

crinkling his forehead. I checked the clock: It wasn't even noon, and I was supposed to be with Portia and Zane until one.

I paced the store restlessly as I told Dad and Mason what had happened.

"Logan knew how important today was," I finished. "This was the first song we really created as a team. He knew I couldn't play it for Zane without him, and he knew Zane and Portia had high expectations. I don't understand why he didn't let me know he couldn't make it."

Mason shrugged. "Well, you and Logan haven't always seen eye to eye."

"But he wasn't mad at me this time," I insisted. "Besides, that's no reason for him to not show up."

"You're right, but there's not much you can do about it right now," Dad replied.

An idea flew into my mind. "We should drive over to his house to see if he's okay."

Dad sighed wearily. I could already hear the no coming.

"Why not?" I persisted. "You know where Logan lives, and it's not far away."

WHERE ARE YOU?

"I've got deliveries coming," Dad said. "I need to stay here."

"Mason could run me over there in the truck," I suggested.

"I could," Mason admitted.

Dad's mouth tied into a thoughtful bow. "Fine," he relented, "but make it quick."

It only took a few minutes to drive to Logan's house. As Mason pulled up out front, I peered at the house through my window. The curtains were drawn, and the garage was closed.

"Doesn't look like anyone's home," Mason said.

"I need to check," I said.

I hopped out of the truck and walked toward the house along a footpath overgrown with weeds. A smiley face on a worn welcome mat grinned up at me in front of a rusty, lopsided screen door. I rang the doorbell twice, but no one answered.

When I got back in the truck, Mason gave my shoulder a squeeze.

"Don't get stressed about it," he said as I fastened my seat belt.

"I'm not," I replied, but I didn't even convince myself.

On the drive back to Dad's shop, my brain tumbled anxiously over what could have happened to Logan. Had he bailed on me and our music? Or even worse, had he or someone in his family gotten hurt?

When we walked inside the store, Dad was on his phone, his voice low. His face was red and his jaw was hard, the way they get when he's upset. When he saw us, he murmured something into the phone and hung up.

"What's wrong? Is it Logan?" I asked.

Dad nodded. Suddenly, I was too afraid to say anything. A few weeks ago, I wasn't even sure if I liked Logan, but now the thought that he could be hurt froze me with fear.

"What happened?" Mason asked. "Is he okay?"

"Yes and no," Dad said. "Logan didn't make rehearsal because he got arrested."

SILENCE

Chapter 8

I blinked hard, trying to wrap my head around what I'd just heard.

"Logan couldn't have gotten arrested," I insisted. "There must be some mistake."

"It didn't sound like it," Dad said gruffly. "That was Zane on the phone. He told me Logan's been charged with shoplifting."

"I don't understand," I said. "What did he steal? Where?"

Dad shrugged, frowning. "No idea. Zane said he'd call back when he knew more."

My brain felt like it was in a spin cycle of a washing machine. I had so many questions, and Logan was the only person who could answer them.

"I need to talk to Logan," I said, pulling out my phone.

"If he's been arrested, he probably doesn't have his phone right now," Mason pointed out, but I was already texting Logan.

Are you OK? I wrote. The message sent with a *whoosh* and I stared at the screen, waiting for a response.

"Try to be patient, Tenn," Dad said.

"I *am*," I said, pocketing my phone.

My patience lasted for another twelve minutes and nineteen seconds. When Logan still hadn't replied, I sent him a second text asking if he'd gotten my first text. When he didn't reply to either one, I called his cell phone and left a message. There was no answer at his house, either, so I left a message there, too.

The store closed at six. I still hadn't heard from Logan. By the time we drove home, my stomach was churning with sour worry.

At dinner, Logan was the main topic of conversation.

"I have to say, I don't have the faintest idea what he was thinking," Dad said, his voice hard. "Clearly that boy's more trouble than he looks."

SILENCE

I bristled. "Dad, you *know* Logan," I said. "He's a good person."

Dad gave a terse shrug. "Well, maybe he's not the boy we thought he was," he said, wiping his mouth with his napkin.

Heat flooded my cheeks. I knew Dad could be right, but I wasn't ready to give up on Logan. "We don't know the whole story yet," I whispered.

Mom and Dad exchanged a look.

"Maybe not," Mom said, "but until we know more, Dad and I think you should step back from your partnership with Logan."

My head felt like it could explode. "What do you mean, *step back*?" I asked.

"Take a break from each other," Dad said. "No rehearsals together, no songwriting, and definitely no performing."

"Stop playing music with him?" I said in disbelief. "Why? We just wrote a great song together."

"That seems kind of unfair," Mason chipped in. Aubrey nodded in agreement.

"It *is* unfair," I said, my throat tightening. "Logan and I are partners—"

"For the moment," Dad interrupted firmly.

Mom threw him a sharp look.

"What does *that* mean?" I asked Dad, curiosity prickling down my neck.

My parents exchanged another look.

Mom sighed, meeting my gaze. "Zane is very concerned about Logan's arrest," she said. "If Logan broke the law, it wouldn't just damage his own reputation; the bad publicity could also hurt the two of you as a duo. Zane's going to meet with Logan and get the whole story, but he's also going to let him know that he's in danger of being dropped by the label. If that happens, it's possible that Tenney and Logan could be dropped, too."

A chill ran through me, as if all my blood suddenly froze in my veins. I opened my mouth to say something, but nothing came out. I felt like I'd been turned to stone.

"There's no way that will happen," Mason said, squeezing my shoulder reassuringly. "Zane loves Tenney."

"True," Mom said. "But he decided to partner her with Logan when he signed them as a duo."

SILENCE

"I don't understand," I said.

Mom turned to me, her eyes soft with sympathy. "I'm just saying that it's not up to us, honey. He might decide to drop Logan and keep you on the label as a solo act. We just don't know yet."

I gulped. Inside I was a giant whirlpool of emotions—anger, fear, but mostly confusion.

"But Logan and I signed a contract . . ." I trailed off.

"I know, honey," Dad said. "But sometimes this happens in the music business."

"What if Logan and I don't want to break up our act?" I said desperately.

"You might not have a choice," Dad said.

I took a deep breath, my emotions settling into a glob of dull sadness in my stomach. I knew Dad was right—if Zane decided to drop Logan, there was nothing I could do. But then I remembered the pure joy on Logan's face when we'd finished writing "The Nerve." *Music is the best thing in my life,* he had told me. *I won't let anything keep me from playing.* The memory forged a nugget of confidence inside me. No matter what, I thought, Logan would do whatever he could to keep our act together.

"This is all going to turn out to be nothing," I said, trying to reassure myself. "It's just a big mistake."

"Maybe," Dad said, but neither he nor Mom looked convinced. Their expressions made my confidence weaken into doubt.

"I can't believe this is happening," I whispered. Aubrey leaned over in her chair and hugged me, but it just made me feel worse.

"I'm sorry, I need to be excused," I mumbled, and before my parents could reply, I rushed out.

I ran upstairs to my room and curled up on my bed. As soon I was alone, I buried my head in my pillow. I wanted to cry, but I couldn't. I was angry, but I wasn't sure who to be angry with—Logan or Zane or my parents or the whole situation. I turned over, rubbing my eyes, and stared at the ceiling.

We finally found our voice, I thought sadly, *and now it might not matter.*

I didn't want to go back to being a solo act. I'd gotten used to being one half of Tenney & Logan. Thinking about that ending made me feel suddenly, deeply lost. If I felt that way, I couldn't even imagine how Logan would feel when Zane talked to him.

I sat up on the bed and wrapped my arms tight around my knees. I wanted to talk to Logan. I wanted to tell him that our band and our music had come to mean something to me. I wanted to ask him why he would risk losing everything we had worked toward. But I knew I couldn't. I had to wait until he called me back, or until Zane told us his decision. And I had no idea how long that would take.

WHEN THE
MUSIC STOPS

Chapter 9

*T*he next day was Monday, and we still hadn't heard anything from Logan or Zane by the time I got home from school. After I had finished my homework, I was restless, circling the kitchen like a song on repeat.

"Honey, try to do something constructive," Mom suggested as she rolled out a mound of biscuit dough. I shook my head.

"I can't focus on anything right now," I said.

"Okay, then make yourself useful and walk the dog," Mom said. She pulled Waylon's leash off a row of hooks on the wall. Waylon immediately jumped up and started wagging his tail.

"Fine," I said with a sigh, taking the leash.

I'd hoped that walking Waylon would calm me down, but I couldn't stop thinking about Logan.

WHEN THE MUSIC STOPS

Why hadn't he called me yet? I had no idea if he didn't have a phone or was angry with me and wanted to be left alone. Even if I couldn't speak with Logan, I needed to talk to someone who could understand how I was feeling. Before I knew it, Waylon and I had walked the nine blocks to Portia's cottage.

She looked surprised to see us when she opened the door, but she let us in. She fixed Waylon a bowl of water and me a glass of sweet tea, and we got comfortable in the sitting room.

"How're you holding up?" Portia asked with a sad, concerned smile.

"Not good," I said miserably. "Have you heard anything about Logan?"

"Not yet," she said. "I know this must be confusing to you."

"It is," I said. "Logan was proud of our song, and he was excited that we were going to open for Belle Starr. Why would he risk all that by shoplifting?" I tucked my legs up under me. "I just don't think we know the whole story. It makes no sense."

Portia raised an eyebrow. "A lot of things in

this world don't make sense," she observed.

"This is different," I said. I clenched my hands together as I struggled to put my feelings into words. "I just know how much playing music helps Logan. It's like breathing to him—he *has* to do it. Remember how you said music helped heal you after your stroke?" I reminded her. "I can tell it's like that for him, too. Right now he needs music more than ever. That's why I think we should go over to his house and talk to him."

Portia set her chin in her hand. "A couple of weeks ago you couldn't even be in the same room with Logan for five minutes before you had fire shooting out of your ears," she said. "Why do you want to help him now?"

I heard our duet playing in my head, and the answer flooded into my heart.

"When I first met Logan, I thought that he was selfish," I explained. "Since I've gotten to know him, I've realized he's not. He might not always be sweet as pie, but I know he cares about our music as much as I do," I finished passionately. "There's no way I can give up on our music. Which means there's no way I can give up on him."

Portia leaned back in her chair and studied me. It was tough to tell what she was thinking. But just as my heart began to sink into hopelessness, she spoke.

"Okay then," she said. "Let's go talk to Logan."

Portia drove a classic Ford truck with a big curved hood, the kind you see in old movies. It swayed as she turned off the main road onto Logan's street. I pointed out his house, and she parked out front.

"Okay," she said. "You ready?"

I nodded, but I was nervous.

When we'd dropped Waylon at home, I'd expected that I'd have to beg Mom to let me go with Portia to see Logan, but to my surprise she gave me permission.

"I agree that you need to talk to Logan," she'd said gently. "Just remember, Tenney, things don't always turn out the way we want them to."

TENNEY SHARES THE STAGE

Mom's words echoed in my head as Portia and I walked up the overgrown path to Logan's house. I rang the doorbell.

After a moment, a little boy opened the door. He had on a T-shirt, jeans, and a red sheet tied around his neck like a cape. His hair was sandy like Logan's but spiky as a hedgehog. Thick eyeglasses were strapped around his head with a purple elastic band.

"Hi!" he said, almost yelling.

"Oh! Hi," Portia said, startled. She squinted at him like he was an alien.

"Is Logan here?" I asked.

The boy shook his head vigorously. "He went to the grocery store," he said.

"Are you his brother?" I guessed. The boy nodded shyly, but when I smiled at him, he smiled back.

"I'm Jude," he said.

There was a noise behind him. Logan's mom stepped into the doorway. She looked like she'd just woken up.

"Portia, Tenney," she said blearily. "What are you doing here?"

WHEN THE MUSIC STOPS

"I was hoping to talk to Logan," I said.

Mrs. Everett nodded. "Y'all have to forgive me," she said. "I got home about an hour ago from working a night shift at the hospital. Logan took his bike to go run an errand."

"Can we wait for him?" I asked.

Mrs. Everett looked surprised, but with a nod she opened the door wider to let us in the house.

The Everetts' living room was tidy but sort of bare, with a flowery rug and a wall of framed photos above a fraying couch. Jude plopped himself down by a pile of toys on the rug and zoomed a little train around the floor. The rest of us got settled, then stared at one another, as if we'd forgotten whose turn it was to go next.

"How's Logan?" Portia asked, breaking the silence.

"Pretty upset," said Mrs. Everett. "After we got home from the station, I gave him a piece of my mind. Then Zane came over and did the same thing. It wasn't what Logan wanted to hear," she said, folding her arms, "but he needed to hear it. What he did was wrong."

TENNEY SHARES THE STAGE

"So he really shoplifted?" I said, a chill running through me.

She nodded. Her expression was serious. My heart went cold, like it had been plunged into ice water. I'd convinced myself that Logan's arrest must have been a misunderstanding of some kind. Now I didn't know what to think.

"Can you tell us what happened?" Portia asked.

"Of course," Mrs. Everett said with a tired sigh. She took a deep breath. "Logan's a great kid," she began. "He's helpful, loyal, and he prides himself on being independent. But he's also stubborn. He thinks he can handle more than he should sometimes. And since his dad's been gone, he's had to take on a lot more responsibility than most kids his age."

"My dad's in Japan playing guitar with Godzilla!" Jude shouted. He let out a T. rex–sized roar and ran into the kitchen. His silliness broke the tension for a moment, and we all smiled.

"Phil's been on tour backing a Japanese band for a while now, but the pay has been unpredictable," Mrs. Everett said. "Last month the band told him they weren't going to pay him till the end of the tour. Because of that, it's been tough to get our bills paid on time."

"I've been there," Portia said.

Mrs. Everett gave a hard nod, but her eyes softened. "Music is my husband's life," she continued. "I knew that when I married him. I just wish it was a little bit easier."

"How long is he on tour for?" I asked.

Mrs. Everett's lower lip trembled. She glanced at Jude in the kitchen and lowered her voice to a whisper. "I'm not sure," she finally said. "He had a rough time getting work in Nashville. And since he went on tour he's been sending checks home, so we're grateful." She shifted uncomfortably. "You see, money's been tight for a while. Even when Logan's dad was sending us money, I had to pick up extra shifts at work. So Logan's been helping out more at home, and with his brother. He even got a job."

"A job?" Portia said. "He's only fourteen."

"It was his choice," Logan's mom said. "When he told me he wanted to find a job, I discouraged him. I wanted him to focus on music and school. Most of all, I didn't want him to feel responsible for our family. But he begged and begged until I gave in. He took on a few hours a week as a junior custodian at the hospital where I work." She shook her head, almost like she was angry. Then she let out a long, sad sigh. "It was a mistake. Lately he's been trying to balance school, music, a job, and helping out at home. He won't admit it, but of course he's been overwhelmed."

Suddenly, all of Logan's strange behavior—his bad moods and lateness, the moments when he constantly checked his phone, and the times when he rushed out of our songwriting sessions—started to make sense to me. *Logan wasn't being a jerk,* I realized. *He's just been trying to keep up with everything.*

Jude rushed back into the room with a juice box and flopped down beside his mother. She kissed his head and let out a wobbly breath.

"Looking back, I see now that Logan was getting stressed out," she said, "but he never talked to me about it. Then yesterday we found out that Logan's dad wants to stay in Japan for as long as he has work, which could be until the end of the year," she explained. "Logan was upset, but he didn't want to talk about it. I'd worked the night shift, so I was exhausted. The plan was for Logan to watch Jude and let me sleep for a couple of hours, and then he would leave and meet y'all for rehearsal," she continued. "But clearly that didn't happen."

"What did?" I asked.

"I hadda azzma 'tack!" Jude proclaimed proudly. He stood up in a superhero pose.

Mrs. Everett smiled sadly and put her arms around him. "Jude has asthma," she explained. "He was having trouble breathing, and he'd used up his inhaler medication. Instead of waking me up, Logan decided to go to the pharmacy to get an inhaler refill for Jude on his own. Unfortunately, his bike had a flat tire, so he ran the whole way there. When he finally got to the pharmacy, he asked for the order and then realized he'd forgotten his wallet at home and didn't have his money or our insurance card. The pharmacist told Logan that he'd have to come back for the medication. But then she went to answer a phone call, leaving the medication sitting there on the counter . . ."

"And Logan took it," Portia finished.

Mrs. Everett nodded and wiped a tear from the corner of her eye. "The pharmacist alerted security, and a guard stopped him before he got out the door. Logan told the guard that his plan was to go get the money and come right back with it, but of course that's no excuse. He was tired and worried about Jude and frustrated and he made a horrible decision."

She shook her head, as if she still couldn't quite believe what had happened. "Then the police called me to come and pick him up," she said. "It looks like they may drop the shoplifting charge if he does some community service . . ." She trailed off and suddenly looked up at us with fierce eyes. "I just want to make sure y'all know that what Logan did isn't who he is as a person. He's better than that."

"I know he is," I replied firmly. I was actually a little relieved—Logan may have broken the law, but he was just trying to help his little brother.

The front door clicked open. Logan walked in

holding a bag of groceries. He froze as soon as he saw Portia and me.

"What are they doing here?" he asked, his voice wavering.

"Portia and Tenney came to see how you're doing, honey," his mom said.

Portia nodded. "We're sorry you've been going through a rough time."

Logan turned bright red. "I'm fine," he said gruffly.

As he started for the kitchen, I jumped up. "I'm really ..." I began. I wanted to say *I'm really glad you're okay.* But Logan had just been through something awful, and might not *feel* okay. So instead I said, "I'm really sorry you missed rehearsal."

Logan gave me a hard look. "I have to put the groceries away," he growled under his breath. He turned his back on me and went into the kitchen.

I stood there uncertainly. Logan seemed so angry—but why? I was a little afraid to talk to him, but I also felt like I *had* to talk to him. Portia gave me an encouraging nod. *Tell him how you feel,* her eyes seemed to say.

TENNEY SHARES THE STAGE

I took a deep breath and followed Logan into the kitchen.

He was unpacking groceries at the counter when I came in.

"Hey," I said.

He glowered at me and folded up the paper grocery bag.

"I've been trying to call you," I said. "I tried your cell a bazillion times yesterday."

"Good for you," Logan said, his voice as sharp as a razor. He whipped open a cabinet, shoved some soup cans onto a shelf, and slammed it closed.

"Why are you angry?" I asked.

Logan whirled around to face me, eyes blazing with suspicion.

"Did you tell Portia what I told you about my family?" he said accusingly.

"No," I said, caught off guard.

Logan scoffed, and I bristled.

"I didn't tell her anything," I insisted.

"Then why is she here?" he demanded. "Why did she say that she was sorry I've been going through a rough time?"

"She's here because you got arrested,"
I hissed. I felt bad as soon as I said it. I knew
rubbing Logan's mistake in his face wasn't going
to make anything better.

I breathed in and out, trying to calm myself.
"Logan, I'm sorry your family's been having a hard
time," I said at last.

"Like you understand," he muttered.

His words sliced me like a blade. "What does
that mean?" I snapped.

Logan yanked a gallon of milk off the counter
and put it in the fridge. "It means your family's
perfect, okay? You all play music together and your
dad's here and you're really talented and you've
never really had to struggle for anything," he said.
"I seriously doubt you understand anything I've
been going through. And now you brought Portia
here." He took a long breath and threw me a sharp
look. "I thought I could trust you."

My jaw clenched as I fought to keep my temper
from getting away from me. "I didn't tell Portia anything," I repeated, "because I didn't *know* anything.
You never trusted me enough to tell me what was

going on. Maybe if you had, none of this would have happened!"

"Why, because you would have fixed everything?" Logan shot back.

"I could have helped," I said.

"I don't *need* your help!" he said, spitting out the words. "I don't need anyone's help."

"Yes, you do, and your family does, too," I insisted.

Logan's lips trembled, but he just shrugged. I waited for him to say something, but he didn't.

"Your mom told us everything—about your dad in Japan and your job at the hospital. Why didn't you tell me what was really going on?" I asked.

He hesitated, gritting his teeth. "Because you would have treated me differently," he finally said.

"That's not true!" I replied.

"You can't say that for sure," he said. "I didn't want you knowing that I was leaving rehearsal to go clean toilets at night. And that I didn't write songs because I had to do laundry and dishes and put Jude to bed. I didn't want it to affect the band."

WHEN THE MUSIC STOPS

"But it did," I said gently. "How can we be partners if you don't let me in? Logan, we're in this together."

"I know!" Logan said, like that was the dumbest thing I'd ever said.

"You're not acting like it!" I shot back, frustration making my voice rise. "What happens to your music career happens to mine, too. I might lose my deal with Mockingbird because of this, and that's totally unfair."

I paused. I knew I'd sounded selfish, and Logan looked hurt, but I didn't care. *It's the truth,* I thought. *He needs to hear it.*

"So that's what you care about. Losing your record deal," Logan said, shaking his head.

I struggled to keep my voice cool. "That's not *all* I care about," I replied, "but it's part of it. Don't you even care that Zane might cancel our contract?"

Logan's ears turned bright red and his mouth clenched, but he said nothing. I blinked, aggravation rising in my chest.

"Aren't you even going to apologize?" I asked.

"No," he snapped. "I was doing what I needed to do for my family."

"I know, but this isn't just about you," I said. "It affects our music and our future. You can't pretend these things aren't connected. We're a team. I'm a part of your life now, too."

"I never asked you to be a part of my life," Logan shot back.

His words stung, and my face turned hot with embarrassment. For a second Logan looked like he regretted what he'd said, but he turned away quickly.

"Okay," I said slowly. "If you feel that way then maybe we shouldn't play together anymore."

"Fine, if that's what you want," Logan said tersely. "I'll tell Zane I'm done."

It felt as if he'd pushed me as hard as he could. I leaned against the wall, my knees turning to jelly, and stared at Logan's back. I wanted him to turn around so I could tell him, *That's not what I want. I want us to be partners who trust each other. I want us to get through this.*

But he didn't turn around. So I didn't say it.

WHEN THE MUSIC STOPS

I felt like a ghost as I walked back to the living room, shadowy and fragile. Portia was talking to Mrs. Everett, but it was like they were a million miles away, on some far-off moon. When Logan appeared in the kitchen doorway, I looked at a wall instead of at his face because there was no way I was going to cry in front of him. I stood there waiting to leave, looking at nothing as my emotions swirled together until all I felt was lost.

DUET FOR ONE

Chapter 10

"*I* can't believe Logan actually quit yesterday," Jaya said, her brown eyes wide and stunned.

"He did," I said.

Holliday, who was sitting across the lunch table from us, exchanged a concerned glance with Jaya. "He'll probably change his mind," she said uncertainly.

It was exactly what Portia had said when I told her. Mom had said, "Give Logan some time," and Dad had told me not to think about it until we talked to Zane. But Aubrey had almost cried when she heard, and Mason's face had darkened into an angry storm cloud.

"It's Logan's loss," he'd said, giving me a hug. "You don't need him, anyway."

I wasn't sure if I believed that, but the day

after my fight with Logan, I'd woken up sure of one thing: "Even if Logan wasn't serious about quitting," I told Jaya and Holliday, "after the way he acted, I don't ever want to perform with him again."

"Of course not!" Jaya said, putting a protective arm around me.

Holliday leaned her chin in her hand. "That's too bad," she said. "You guys sounded great together."

"So what? He treated Tenney badly," Jaya said, her voice rising in indignation.

"I know," Holliday said slowly. "But it also sounds like he was embarrassed. I know that sometimes when I get upset or feel bad about myself, it comes out as anger, and I end up saying things I regret."

Her blue eyes met mine. I knew she was thinking about all the times she'd been mean to me, before we were really friends. "I'm not saying it's okay," Holliday continued, "but I understand a bit why Logan might have acted how he did. Right now, you're upset, but if you step back and think about it, you might feel that way, too."

"Maybe," I said doubtfully.

But Holliday's suggestion stayed with me as we threw out our lunch trash. Throughout the afternoon, I thought back to my fight with Logan. I wasn't proud of how I'd lost my temper with him. I couldn't help but wonder if he felt the same way.

After school, my parents took me downtown to meet with Zane and Ellie Cale and find out whether I had a future at Mockingbird Records. The whole way there I was jittery, like I was sitting on a carpet of pins. I tried to clear my mind, but I kept hearing Zane's voice telling me he was going to end my contract. By the time we settled ourselves on the wide leather couches in Zane's office, I was a fragile bubble of emotion.

"Well, I spoke to Logan," Zane said, rubbing his neck, "and he confirmed he's quitting. I'm really sorry, Tenney."

"Oh," I said quickly. The tiny glimmer of hope

I still had left for Tenney & Logan snuffed out inside me. I blinked, dazed. My brain felt like it was rolled in bubble wrap, but my heart was raw with sadness. I felt lost and afraid.

And I had no idea if Zane wanted to keep me on his label.

"What does this mean for me?" I asked Zane, my voice quavering. "Do you still want to work with me?"

"Are you kidding? Of course!" Zane said with a grin. "You're very talented, Tenney," he continued. "I've thought about it, and I believe we can reposition you as a solo act, possibly with a small backing band."

For a moment my heart zinged with relief. But for some strange reason, I wasn't as happy as I thought I'd be.

"What about the contract she signed with Logan?" Mom asked, frowning.

"I've already talked to our lawyers about drawing up a new recording contract for Tenney as a solo artist," Ellie responded. "It'll take a few days, but once you all sign off on it, the other contract with Logan will be automatically terminated. How does that sound, Tenney?"

"That sounds okay," I replied uncertainly. "But what's Logan going to do now?"

Zane hesitated. "I think he might take a break," he said. "He made it clear that he doesn't want to pursue a professional music career right now."

"Oh," I said. While a small part of me was excited that I was finally getting the solo recording contract I had always dreamed of, I mostly felt sad and even a little guilty that Logan had quit.

I think Mom could tell I was upset, because she put an arm around me. For a moment, my heart steadied.

Then I remembered something.

"What about our performance at Riff's?" I asked. "Logan and I were supposed to open for Belle Starr next weekend. That's not enough time to put together a great solo set."

"We agree," Ellie said reassuringly. "We'll send our regrets. Belle will understand. And there will be plenty of big opportunities like that in the future."

Zane nodded. "The most important thing right now is to focus on your music," he told me. "As a start, I want you to go back through the set that you and Logan put together, play each song, and think about which ones you want to keep in your solo set," he said. "Logan told me you could go ahead and keep playing the song you wrote together. What's it called?"

"'The Nerve,'" I replied.

"Right. Logan said it's a good song, and he'd be happy if you performed it," Zane said. "He said you could revise the lyrics if you want."

A sour feeling rose in my stomach. It was nice of Logan to let me play the song, but somehow the idea of performing it without him made me feel even worse.

"You don't have any upcoming gigs booked yet," Zane finished. "So right now I'd just take a moment and think about what *you* want out of your musical career."

I nodded, but inside I was still a puddle of mixed emotions.

Ellie gave me an encouraging smile. "I know

this feels strange," she said, "but try to think of it as an opportunity for you to move forward."

But what if I'm scared to move forward without Logan? I thought.

As we walked to the door, all I could think of was Logan. Playing music was his dream, just like it was mine. I couldn't believe he was giving all that up because of our fight.

"Did Logan tell you anything about why he quit?" I asked Zane.

Zane hesitated, then nodded. "He said he didn't want to hold you back."

I spent that night and much of the next day lost in my thoughts about Logan and our music and my future. I walked to Dad's shop after school, did my homework, and surfed the Internet in the storeroom until Dad poked his head in.

"Aren't you going to practice today?" he asked.

"I don't know," I said. Normally I love playing guitar, but right now the idea made me uneasy.

DUET FOR ONE

"I'm not sure how it will feel to play the songs without Logan," I admitted.

"Well, sweetheart, it will probably feel a little uncomfortable," Dad said gently. "But you're going to have to face it sometime."

He was right, of course. And I knew I should get to work on figuring out my solo set, as Zane had requested. I grabbed my songwriting journal from my bag and my guitar from behind the register and headed to the listening room.

As I closed the door, a memory flashed in my mind of the first time Logan and I played "The Nerve" all the way through while standing across from each other in this little room. It had felt like we could do anything, even fly. I'd been sure he'd felt the same way . . . and yet here I was now, alone.

I sat on a stool and leaned against the wood paneling, settling my guitar on my knees. I put my journal on the music stand in front of me, opening it to the page where I'd written the set list for our Cumberland Park performance.

I really didn't want to play through each song. But I reminded myself that being a professional means practicing even when you don't feel like it, so that was what I was going to do.

I started working through the set list. The first song was "Reach the Sky." I'd originally written it as a solo, so I knew how it could be played that way. The next few numbers were tougher. Logan and I had worked hard to arrange each song with him on drums and me on guitar. As I listened to myself playing, I couldn't help but shake my head. The melodies sounded fragile when performed alone. I could *hear* Logan's absence. More than that, I could *feel* it—a drab, lonely emptiness that was worse than silence.

Just keep going, I told myself, moving to the next song, "Where You Are." I played it all the way through without much joy. It didn't sound bad exactly, but in my mind I kept hearing the way the music had sounded when Logan and I played it together.

I checked the next song on the list. "The Nerve." It was a true duet, equal parts mine and Logan's. Just thinking about performing it without him felt wrong, even if he had given me permission to do it. *How would I feel if he performed it without me?* I wondered. I'd be angry and heartbroken for sure. But I'd promised Zane that I would try playing all the songs on my own. So, even though it made my heart hurt, I forced myself to start.

After only three measures, I had to stop.

I didn't know how to play "The Nerve" without Logan, I realized, and more important, I didn't want to. I didn't want to sing his lines about the things about me that annoyed him. And I didn't want to sing the final chorus, when we express how great we are together. Playing it alone would just remind me how much better it sounded when Logan and I were performing together.

I put down my guitar and wrapped my arms around my knees. A tear slipped down my cheek. I wiped it away and reminded myself that I was working with an amazing producer on great music that I had written, with the promise of recording a possible solo album. I was on the verge of getting everything I'd always wanted.

But without Logan, everything felt wrong. Our duet felt broken without him and so did I. Why?

Because I'm still not ready to give up on him, I realized.

I wanted Logan to know that I still believed in our music. But how could I convince him to believe in us again? The last time I'd tried talking to him, it had ended beyond horribly.

As I drew in a sad breath, a lyric formed in my head. It was familiar and new at the same time, and it expressed exactly what I was feeling. I grabbed my pen and flipped my journal open to a blank page. I'd barely jotted down the lyric before a melody floated in behind it.

I picked up my guitar and started playing the melody filling my head. There are moments when the music in my head is so loud it feels like my brain might explode if I don't play it. It felt like that now.

By the time Dad popped his head in and told me to get ready to go home, I'd gotten most of the song down on paper. The lyrics were rough, but writing down everything I wanted to tell Logan had made me feel a lot better. For now, that had to be enough.

THE SEARCH

Chapter 11

*F*or the rest of the week, I worked on my song about Logan whenever I got the chance. I'd plow through my homework at Dad's shop, then shut myself in the listening room with my guitar until closing time. Sometimes writing a song is hard for me, other times it's easy. With this song, I knew exactly what I wanted to tell Logan, but I couldn't figure out the best words to express it.

I'd sit on the floor of the listening room with my songwriting journal open to the lyrics. Playing the song felt like trying to figure out a musical puzzle. As I strummed the chords, the lyrics would shift around in my mind across the melody line. When I hit a bumpy moment, I'd switch words to better fit the music, or stretch out the music to support the lyrics. Then I'd start over from the top. It was hard work, but each time the music and lyrics fit together a little more smoothly.

By Saturday morning, the song felt like an old friend, easy and familiar. *Not bad,* I thought to myself as I strummed the final notes on the back porch after breakfast. Logan might never hear the song I'd written for him, but writing it had given me hope.

A ripple of claps rang out behind me, and I jumped. My parents stood on the porch behind me. I'd been so focused I hadn't even heard them come out.

"Good song! Is it new?" Mom asked.

I nodded shyly. "It's sort of inspired by the whole Logan thing," I said.

Dad's eyebrows raised, but Mom didn't seem surprised.

"I know you wish things had worked out differently," she said.

I nodded, a lump of mixed emotions crowding my throat. "I've been thinking maybe I should call Logan," I said.

Dad's mouth creased into a disapproving

line, but I stayed focused on Mom.

After a moment's hesitation, she nodded. "Sure," she told me. "There's no reason you can't still be friends."

"Exactly," I said, my brain whirling. "We could even jam together sometimes!"

My parents exchanged a concerned look.

"Well, you can play together at some point," Mom said carefully. "But remember, honey, Logan quit. We agree with Zane that, right now, you need to be focused on your own music."

"Yep," Dad agreed. "You don't need to be working with someone who's less committed to music than you are."

Irritation prickled up my back. "Logan's not less committed to music than I am," I said.

"Well, he's more troubled," Dad shot back.

I bit my tongue, knowing there was nothing I could say that would change Dad's mind about Logan. He had clearly decided that Logan was a bad seed, and Mom wasn't in a rush to argue with him about it.

"In any case," Dad told me, "Zane just e-mailed

me a draft of your new contract. Our lawyer has to look at it, but hopefully we'll be able to sign it by next week. Then you'll officially be a solo act. Something to look forward to!"

"Right," I managed, but as Mom hugged me, my insides were churning.

An hour later, Mom, Dad, and Aubrey left to take the food truck to a street fair in Franklin. Mason stayed home to rewire a speaker in the garage while I worked on my music. Well, I was *supposed* to be working on music. Instead, I was staring at a wall with my guitar in my lap, thinking.

I have to talk to Logan once more before I sign my solo contract, I realized. *I don't have much time left.*

I tried calling him, but his phone wasn't on. I even sent him a text message marked URGENT. No reply. After an hour of waiting, I came up with a new plan of action.

I headed to the garage. Mason didn't exactly look excited to see me, but I was on a mission.

"I need your help," I told him. "I have to talk to Logan face-to-face and clear the air before I sign my solo contract. It's only fair after how hard we worked together. Right now might be my only chance. Can you drive me to see him?"

Mason had our parents' permission to use the pickup for emergencies. I knew this wasn't *officially* an emergency, but it felt like one to me.

Mason crossed his arms, on guard. "Maybe. Where is he?"

"That's the problem," I said, wincing. "I kind of have no idea."

Mason's eyebrows knit together. "So what do you want me to do? Just drive you around Nashville looking for him?"

"Not *all* around Nashville," I said. "Just a few places."

Mason groaned.

"I'll do your chores for a week," I offered.

"Really?" Mason said, perking up. He hates chores. Still, he didn't seem totally convinced yet. "Okay, say you find Logan. What makes you think he's going to want to talk to you?"

I hadn't really considered that.

"He might not," I admitted. "But I have to at least try to get him to listen. Please, Mason."

TENNEY SHARES THE STAGE

"Fine," Mason grumbled. "You have an hour, that's it."

An hour to find Logan somewhere in Nashville and change his mind about everything, I thought, staring out the window as Mason backed down our driveway. *No pressure.*

Our first stop was Logan's house. It looked like no one was home, but I rang the doorbell a few times just in case. No answer.

Next, I directed Mason to Logan's middle school, a few blocks away.

"It's Saturday," Mason said with a frown. "Why would he be at school?"

"Who knows, maybe he has a soccer game or something," I said, even though I didn't think Logan even played soccer. "I just want to make sure."

No one was at the school. We checked the neighborhood library and the park next to it, too. No Logan.

"His mom said he was working part time at a hospital," I said.

"Which one?" Mason replied.

"I don't know," I admitted. "Maybe we should

drive by some of them."

Mason looked at me like I'd suggested we fly to the moon. "Are you kidding? There are at least four hospitals in Nashville. No way," he declared. "This is a waste of time. You should keep calling and texting Logan. Maybe he'll respond just to get you to shut up."

I started to protest, but Mason cut me off.

"Tenney, your hour's almost up already," he said. "We're going home."

I slumped in my seat as Mason turned onto a wide avenue. My heart sank, but I knew it was pointless to argue with him. After a few blocks, I closed my eyes, listening to the sweeping whisper of the truck's tires on the road. As we rolled to a stop, I looked out the window.

We were sitting at a red light at a large intersection. A giant gray building framed by trees stretched to the right. WOODLAND MEMORIAL HOSPITAL, read the sign out front. My gaze flicked over a nearly empty bike rack nearby. Suddenly, my breath caught in my throat.

An orange-and-silver bike was locked to the

rack. Its front tire looked worn and a little deflated. Logan's bike!

Before I could say anything, the traffic light changed green.

"Wait! Stop! Logan's in there!" I said as Mason drove past the hospital entrance.

"What are you talking about?" he asked.

"I saw his bike," I said, hitching my thumb over my shoulder. "I know he's in there."

Mason didn't look happy, but clearly he believed me because he flipped on the truck's blinker and turned around.

We found a spot in the hospital parking lot and hurried into the hospital. Inside the lobby, we studied a wall directory. The place was huge, with dozens of departments.

"If Logan's working, he could be anywhere," Mason said, frowning.

I scanned the directory. "Mrs. Everett is a nurse in the pediatric ward," I said. "Maybe we should start there. At the very least, she'll know where to find Logan."

"That's on the fourth floor," Mason said,

checking the list. "Let's go."

We took the elevator up. When the doors opened, we stepped out into a long curving hall decorated with bright paintings of animals. A short distance away, a nurse in hospital scrubs sat behind a wide purple admissions desk.

"Excuse me," I said as we stepped up to the desk. "We're looking for Nurse Everett."

The nurse typed a few letters and squinted at her screen. "Sorry, hon," she said, looking up at me. "Marlene isn't working until later today."

"What about her son, Logan?" Mason said.

I nudged him and gave him a look. I didn't want Logan to know we were looking for him in case he might try to avoid us.

The nurse looked back at her screen. "Looks like his shift just ended down the hall. Do you want me to page him for you?"

"No!" I said, catching myself. "I mean, we'll just talk to him later."

She nodded, and then got distracted as a doctor came up to talk to her. I took off down the hallway, and Mason followed me.

TENNEY SHARES THE STAGE

We passed through a big set of swinging doors. The hall ahead was lined with seemingly endless doors, each leading to a hospital room.

"I don't think we're allowed to be in here," Mason whispered as we walked past doors.

"I haven't seen any signs saying we can't," I replied, scanning the hall. "Just try and act like you belong."

Mason rolled his eyes, but he kept walking. We nodded to a passing doctor and moved past a nurse's station, around a curving wall that opened up to a whole new row of rooms. There was still no sign of Logan.

"He's not here," Mason whispered, as we moved past door after door.

"Yes, he is," I insisted. *He has to be,* I thought to myself. *Because if he's not, I don't know what else to do.*

Then I heard something: a silvery, far-off sound that got clearer the moment I stood still.

"Someone's playing guitar," I said. Mason nodded, listening.

I edged forward, following the faint music. Suddenly, my breath froze in my chest.

THE SEARCH

I knew that song. It was one of my songs: "Reach the Sky"!

Mason and I stared at each other. I could tell he'd recognized the song, too. Before we could say anything, we heard Logan's voice singing my lyrics.

"Gonna be myself, nobody else," he sang. "Gonna reach the sky if I only try."

"Why's he singing your song?" Mason asked, reading my mind.

"I don't know," I replied.

We moved toward the music, curiosity pushing us forward. It was coming from the end of the hall. We reached the doorway to a community room marked THE GATHERING PLACE. The door was slightly open. The song was coming from inside.

Mason touched my shoulder. "I'll wait here," he whispered.

I nodded, grateful that he understood I'd want to talk to Logan alone. With a deep breath, I stepped up to the door and slipped inside.

The room was dim and still, with clusters of cozy chairs, couches, and tables; bookshelves lined the walls. The room seemed empty, except for the music. I glanced around for Logan, but I didn't see him. His voice was coming from a tall-backed armchair in a corner of the room.

A little girl sat there, curled up and looking at a tablet. Her small face glowed green in the light.

As I came closer, I realized she was singing along to my song.

ALICE

Chapter 12

*T*he girl looked up. The moment she saw me, she stopped singing. I froze where I was, not wanting to scare her.

She reached over and turned on a lamp to see me better. She looked about Aubrey's age. She was small with short hair tucked behind her ears, and she wore a giant black T-shirt with HARD AS NAILS! scrawled across it in lightning-bolt letters. She had tubes in her nose and an IV attached to her thin arm. Cords led to an oxygen tank and a clear plastic pouch hooked to a rolling cart. She stared at me, the skin under her wide, dark eyes ringed with bluish circles.

"Is my music too loud?" she asked, looking worried. "I can turn it down."

"It's okay," I said, but she'd already pressed a

TENNEY SHARES THE STAGE

button on her tablet, and the music stopped.

"Where did you get that song?" I asked.

The girl gave me a curious look. "My friend Logan recorded it for me," she said. "It's my favorite."

"It is?" I said. I felt my cheeks turn pink. The idea of a song I'd written being someone else's favorite was almost too amazing to imagine. "That's great!" I said, beaming at the girl.

She frowned back at me suspiciously. "I'm Alice," she said. "Who are you?"

"My name's Tenney," I replied.

Alice's eyes grew large. "Logan told me about you!" she piped up, sounding excited. "You're in his band!"

I almost mentioned that we weren't a band anymore, but Alice kept talking.

"I really like your songs," she said. "Logan's played a bunch of them for me! He says you're very talented, but sometimes your pace could be snappier."

She said it exactly the way Logan did when he told me to pick up my tempo. It made me smile.

"How did you meet Logan?" I asked.

"He came to take my breakfast tray from my room one day and he saw my guitar," she said, gesturing toward a chipped guitar leaning against the side table next to her chair. "We started talking about music, and he asked if he could play something for me. He's really good at guitar—a lot better than me."

"Just keep practicing, and someday you'll be even better than Logan," I offered with a smile. "How long have you been playing?"

"Since last year," she said. "I love it."

She looked down at the guitar, her thin face filling with happiness. She leaned over to pick it up, but as she did, she started coughing. It was a sharp, hard sound that shook her whole body, and it didn't stop. She drew her knees up to her chin and held an oxygen mask over her nose and mouth.

I sat down on the couch next to her chair. "Should I get a nurse?" I asked, but Alice shook her head. I couldn't think of what to say, so I just sat there until she was breathing normally again.

She took off the mask and looked up at me.

"I've been to the hospital eleven times," she said in a whisper.

I tried not to look shocked, but I couldn't help it.

Alice's expression turned fierce. "You don't have to feel sorry for me," she said.

I nodded. I'd gone to the hospital for two stitches once when a mandolin string had snapped and hit me in the lip. At the time it had seemed like a big deal. Not anymore.

"Why are you here?" Alice asked. Then her face brightened, and she started talking so fast that I couldn't fit in a single word. "Did Logan tell you I wanted to meet you? This is so great! You have to play something for me. Please?"

Her eyes were flames of hope on her pale face. I couldn't say no.

"Um, sure," I said.

Alice leaned over again and grabbed her guitar by the neck. For a second it seemed too heavy for her as she tried to swing it around the table. I scrambled to grab it and bumped my knee on a table leg, sending a small pile of books slapping to the floor.

Mason popped his head in.

ALICE

"Everything okay? I heard some noise," he said to me.

"We're fine," I said, embarrassed. "Alice, this is my brother, Mason."

Mason gave an awkward wave from the doorway.

"You can come in," Alice said. "Tenney's going to play me a song."

As Mason came over, I slipped the guitar strap over my head and tuned the strings.

"Okay, Alice," I said, standing up to face her and Mason. "Here's a new song that I guarantee Logan hasn't played for you."

Settling my left hand on the frets and my right over the strings, I breathed in and started playing "Someone Who Believes." The intro was soft and gentle, but as I sang, my voice was strong.

Pen and paper in my hand
Just so you can understand
I believe we have a voice
I believe we have a song
The stage is right where we belong

TENNEY SHARES THE STAGE

Alice watched me intently. When I took a breath, so did she. I started the chorus.

> *I am chasing this dream of mine*
> *I just need*
> *Someone who believes*
> *Someone who believes*

Alice's small hands gripped the arms of her chair, but otherwise she sat still, listening as I continued through the next verse.

> *I know that getting there's not easy*
> *We'll never know unless we try*
> *If we just give up all that we love*
> *We'll let the moment pass us by*

I'd just started the bridge when I heard a voice behind me say my name.

My hand skittered off the strings as I looked over my shoulder. Logan stood in the community room doorway. He was wearing blue work coveralls, and he looked pretty shocked to see me.

"Logan!" Alice said as he walked in. "I met Tenney!"

"I see that," Logan said, eyeing me. "What are you doing here?" he asked me, lowering his voice to a growl.

"I needed to talk to you," I said, meeting his eyes.

He looked curious, but Alice interrupted before I could explain.

"This is great!" she said to Logan and me. "Now you can sing 'Reach the Sky' together!"

I expected Logan to say no, but he just looked at me.

"I'll sing it if you will," I told him with an encouraging smile. "You can sing lead. I've heard you sing it on Alice's tablet, so I know you've got the words down."

Logan flushed bright red. "Um, okay," he stammered.

I handed him the guitar, and we sat on the couch so Logan could be beside Alice. He settled the guitar on his knee, leaned forward, and started the opening chords to "Reach the Sky."

"I am planted in the ground, tiny like a seed," he sang to her. "Someday I will make you proud. I'll be steady like a tree. Will you teach me how to grow?"

As he sang, his eyes drifted to mine. I couldn't tell what he was feeling, but I chimed in, harmonizing with him on the chorus. "Gonna be myself, nobody else. Gonna reach the sky if I only try."

I shut my eyes, focusing on our voices blending. We sounded the way we had when we'd performed at Cumberland Park, I thought—in tune and united. So much had happened since then. If only we could go back and try again from the beginning.

I opened my eyes. Logan was watching me. This time when I smiled at him, he smiled back. *We sound good*, I told him silently, and his eyes warmed like he understood.

As he started the measure leading into the second verse, Logan gave me a sharp nod, letting me know he wanted me to sing lead this time. I let my voice ring out, soaring through the lyrics. Then we harmonized again on the chorus, our voices weaving together. From chorus to bridge to chorus, we passed the melody line back and forth as we sang, sharing the song better than we ever had before.

There was a breath of silence when we finished, until Alice's tiny claps broke the quiet.

"That was so good!" Alice piped up, beaming at us. "I wish I could see you guys in concert."

Logan darted a glance at me. "Yeah, well . . ." he trailed off. "I really gotta get home," he said, standing up.

"Wait! Logan . . ." I started.

He looked down at me and tightened his jaw. This was my chance to talk to him, but now that we were face-to-face, doubt crept inside me like a chill. I'd felt horrible when Logan had quit. How would I feel now if I told him I wanted to get back together and he said no?

I blinked hard, and Portia's advice echoed through my mind: *It doesn't matter if it's hard—you have to be honest, say what you feel, and trust that your partner's going to listen with open ears.*

"Can I talk to you?" I said to Logan, before I could chicken out.

He flushed an uncomfortable pink but nodded.

TENNEY SHARES THE STAGE

"I've got to get home to take care of Jude, though," he said. "So I only have a minute."

Mason picked up Alice's guitar. "Why don't you two go for a walk," he said. "I'll keep Alice company." She grinned.

Logan and I went into the hallway. We silently fell into step, both of us staring at the speckled green floor tiles. I didn't know how to start, so I just watched the circus of painted animals pass by on the walls.

At the end of the hall was a small sitting area with a view of downtown. We stood by the window and both started talking at once.

"Listen—" I began, just as Logan said, "I'm sorry."

I blinked, stunned. I'd never thought he'd begin by apologizing. "I'm sorry, too," I said.

"You don't need to be sorry. You were trying to help," he replied, shaking his head. "I just over-reacted. You came over with Portia, and I was so humiliated and mad at myself for messing up . . ." He trailed off, taking a deep, sad breath. "I know you don't only care about your music. It was my fault. This whole thing is my fault."

I swallowed hard. "I wish you had told me what was going on, that's all," I said.

"Me, too," Logan mumbled, leaning against the window. "I didn't think you would understand. I mean, your family's perfect."

"I promise, we're *not* perfect," I assured him. "But I do know how lucky I am. I can't imagine how hard it must be to be so far away from your dad."

Logan nodded.

"How are you doing?" I asked him.

Logan shrugged in that way he does. I used to think he shrugged because he didn't care. But now I suddenly understood that he was shrugging because he was upset. He did care. He was just afraid to say it. Instead of nudging him to say more, I stayed quiet until he was ready to keep talking.

"I really miss my dad," he said after a moment. "I keep trying to remind myself that he loves music just as much as I do, and that he had to go on tour because it's his job. But everything's gotten harder since he left. I just kept pushing everything down and trying to ignore how I felt, and trying to work hard and get everything done, but all it did was make me more upset." He took a big, deep breath, like he was coming up for air. "Sometimes I don't even want my dad to come back," he said in a whisper, "because I'm so angry at him for leaving."

His chin quivered, and for a moment I thought he might cry. I didn't know what to say. I'd never been that angry at anyone in my family before. Even when my parents had told me I couldn't perform at the Bluebird Cafe, I hadn't felt like that. Still, I knew how I felt when I was upset, and how I made myself feel better.

"Playing music helps, right?" I told Logan gently. "I mean, I know it doesn't fix anything, but it helps."

"Sometimes," Logan said, studying his feet. "I love rehearsing and performing, but they're both painful on the days when I miss my dad the most."

"You know, you don't have to go through everything alone, even if it feels like it," I told him. "That's the biggest thing I learned from playing music with you."

Logan looked confused. "What do you mean?"

★ ★

ALICE

"Before we started playing together, I thought that being a real singer-songwriter meant that I had to do everything myself," I said. "When we first started playing together, I didn't want you to change a single note I had written. But then I realized that you made my music better. You made *me* better. You taught me that admitting you need help is hard. It takes courage. But when you lean on someone else for support, that makes you both stronger."

Logan put a hand on the window thoughtfully. "I really taught you that?" he finally said.

"Well, maybe not on purpose," I said lightly, and he laughed. "My point is, you can talk to me," I said, nudging him with my shoulder. "Because we're friends. Right?"

"Right," Logan said, his eyes lighting up, as if he was just realizing it. For the first time since I could remember, he broke into a real, wide smile.

Then I did something crazy: I hugged Logan Everett.

And he did something even crazier: He hugged me back!

In that very moment, I realized that although

TENNEY SHARES THE STAGE

I cared about our music, I cared even more about Logan's friendship.

Before I could tell him that, though, he stepped back and blurted out, "I wish we could still play together."

My heart leaped into my throat. "Me, too!" I said, nodding so hard I felt like a bobblehead in a speeding truck. "Maybe we still can ..."

As we walked back to the community room, I told Logan about the solo contract and how I hadn't signed it yet, which meant our Tenney & Logan contract was still valid. "If we tell Zane and our parents we want to keep playing together, they have to listen," I insisted.

But Logan looked doubtful. "Look, Tenney, I love playing music with you," he said. "But Zane needs me to be a hundred and ten percent committed to the band. I don't think I can do that right now. My family needs me too much."

But what about our music? I wanted to shout. But when I saw how sad Logan looked, my frustration evaporated.

"I understand," I said finally. "Even if we're

not a band, we can still play together sometimes, right?"

Logan nodded, looking relieved. "Are you kidding?" he said to me as we entered the doorway of the community room. "I'll perform with you anytime."

"What about next weekend?" Alice shouted to us from across the room.

Mason, Logan, and I looked at her, confused.

Alice sat forward, her face brightening with excitement. "You guys should perform here in the Gathering Place for the kids in the ward!" she declared. "On Saturdays, the nurses get us all together to have lunch and watch a movie, but it's always something we've all seen before. I'll ask Nurse Jim if Tenney and Logan could play instead!"

Before we could even respond, Alice eased herself out of her chair and pressed a button on the wall. In a flash, a round, cheery-looking bearded man in purple scrubs appeared.

"Everything okay, Alice?" he said.

"Yeah, I'm fine," she said. "These are my

friends." She introduced us to Jim, the head nurse, and told him her idea for the concert. Before she'd even finished explaining, he was nodding enthusiastically.

"What a great idea, Alice!" he said. "We're always looking for experiences to give the kids that'll take their minds off being in the hospital. Live music would be amazing! I bet Doctor Farkas would love this idea, too."

"Great," said Alice, beaming. She turned to us. "So will you do it?"

Logan and I glanced at each other and grinned.

"Yes!" we said in perfect harmony.

SECRET PLANS

Chapter 13

I was so happy that Logan and I were
friends again, and so excited by the idea
of performing with him that I practically floated
back to the truck with Mason. It wasn't until
we were driving home that a troubling thought
brought me back to earth.

"What if Mom and Dad won't let me play the
gig with Logan?" I asked Mason.

Mason scoffed. "They will," he said. "It's for a
good cause."

I shook my head, worry rising inside me. "Dad
said he didn't want me performing with Logan."

Mason frowned. "Okay, but you do want to
play with Logan, right?"

"Of course I do!" I said passionately.

"And do you think it's right that Mom and

Dad won't let you perform with him?" Mason persisted.

"No," I admitted. "Logan has a good heart. I want everyone to see that."

"Okay, then," Mason said, with a decisive nod. "So you and I need to come up with a plan."

So we did.

Step one of The Plan began that night at dinner, when Mason and I told our parents about the concert at the hospital. We told them everything about the show ... except that Logan would be there.

"It'll be really low-key," I told them, as we dug into barbecued ribs and corn. "Just thirty or so minutes of music."

"I can go with Tenney and set up her sound equipment," Mason chimed in, giving me a wink.

"Sounds good," Dad said, then turned to me. "How'd you get the gig?"

My stomach tensed, but Mason saved me.

SECRET PLANS

"A friend of a friend asked if she could play," he said.

His explanation was true. Alice *was* the friend of my friend Logan. Still, it made me uncomfortable that I couldn't tell my parents everything yet. If they knew I was planning to perform with Logan, they would put an end to it right away. But I needed to do something to show them why I believed in Logan and our music. *If they see how important this is to me, they'll have to change their minds,* I thought, ignoring the fear cowering in the pit of my stomach.

"Can I play, too?" asked Aubrey, her voice breaking into my thoughts.

I opened my mouth, unsure what to say. Mason gave me a warning glance, but Dad spoke first.

"Why not?" Dad said. "It would be a good experience for you, Aubrey. I mean, as long as Tenney's comfortable with it."

I hesitated. Adding Aubrey would definitely make the show more complicated, but I didn't want to hurt her feelings. I also didn't want to alert my parents that my "low-key" set was anything more than that.

TENNEY SHARES THE STAGE

"Okay," I said to Aubrey. "How about you play the last song with me?"

With a squeal, my sister wrapped me in a hug.

"You won't regret this," she said into my shoulder.

"I hope not," I replied honestly, thinking less about her than everything else still to come.

Step two of The Plan was much easier: invitations. I e-mailed Zane, Ellie, and Portia, asking them to come see me perform at the hospital. I even got the idea to invite Belle Starr as a way of apologizing for having to cancel our opening performance at Riff's. And when I told Jaya and Holliday about the concert after school, they promised to be there—and to keep their lips sealed about Logan.

Step three was rehearsals. Aubrey and I practiced the song we planned to play together every night after dinner. Then I'd go upstairs and video chat with Logan and plan out our set list.

SECRET PLANS

I even managed to slip in a face-to-face rehearsal with Logan at the music store one afternoon when Dad went out to do deliveries and left Mason in charge of the store for a few hours.

Logan and I played through our set list on the low stage, talking through each song. The plan was for both of us to play guitar, alternating who would sing lead. Maybe it was because we hadn't played together in a while, but I'd never had an easier rehearsal with Logan. We were perfectly in tune with each other, musically and otherwise. Without the pressure of writing songs for an EP or making everything perfect for a big-deal show, we were both relaxed, and we plunged together into the joy of making music. By the end of the rehearsal, my face hurt from laughing, and Logan was happier than I'd ever seen him.

As he hung up the guitar he'd been using, sadness passed over his face like a cloud across the sun. "I forgot how much fun this is," he said.

"I know," I said.

Sympathy for Logan surged inside me. *He'd spend every moment playing if he could,* I thought.

If only he knew that this performance could make that possible!

Suddenly, I felt guilty. I hadn't told Logan that Zane, Ellie, and Portia were coming to our concert, because I knew he would refuse to play out of embarrassment and stubbornness. And he didn't know that I hadn't told my parents because I didn't want to tell him that they didn't want me to play with him anymore. But I hoped that by the time I got him to the Gathering Place, Logan would know that he couldn't leave music—or me—behind.

"What's wrong?" Logan asked, squinting at me.

"Nothing," I covered, mustering a smile. "I think we're going to have a great show."

I sounded confident, but that night it was hard to sleep. I felt nervous, wired, and guiltier than ever. Tomorrow, almost everyone close to me would find out I'd been keeping a secret from them.

"At the end of the day, you need to do what's right for your music," Portia had once told Logan and me.

That was what I was doing. I only hoped everyone would understand.

THE GATHERING PLACE

Chapter 14

*T*he next morning I woke with a jolt, as if someone had smashed a gong next to my ears. At breakfast I felt like a bird—fragile, jittery, and ready to fly away—but I forced myself to sit still and eat some oatmeal.

I dressed quickly, putting on a denim vest over a pink T-shirt and my favorite leather skirt. Aubrey was fretting to Mom about getting ready, so I did my hair myself, brushing it into a low side ponytail. I put on my ankle boots and checked my guitar case, making sure I had extra strings and my favorite capo and picks.

Moving to the door, I glanced back at Aubrey sitting on her bed. She chewed her cheek nervously as Mom braided her hair. I could tell she had stage fright already. I remember feeling the same way

TENNEY SHARES THE STAGE

the first time I'd performed in front of an audience.

"You're going to do great, Aubrey," I said.
I gave her an encouraging smile, but she just
nodded and looked at her hands.

"We'll be down in a minute," Mom said gently.

Outside, Mason and Dad were loading cables
and mic stands into the back of Dad's truck.

"Hey, chickadee," Dad said, kissing me on
the cheek as I reached them. "You don't look a bit
nervous."

"I actually am," I admitted. *But not for the
reasons you think*, I added silently.

We weren't scheduled to perform until eleven,
but I'd asked Logan to meet at ten thirty. What
would he say when he saw my parents and Zane
and Portia? Would he storm off—or hear me out?

I was about to run back inside and call Mom
and Aubrey when they appeared. Aubrey was
wearing a pink party dress, but her face looked like
she was going to a funeral.

We piled into Dad's truck and took off, turning onto the broad, shady expanse of Woodland
Avenue. Aubrey sat next to me, resting her chin on

her accordion, her eyes as wide as cymbals.

I didn't feel much better, staring out the window as worst-case scenarios continued to storm inside my head: How would my parents react when they saw Logan there? What if they didn't let me play? What if Logan wanted to come back, but Zane refused to let him?

At last, we pulled up to the hospital. We parked, unloaded the mic stands and cables, and headed inside. When we got out of the elevator on the fourth floor, I spotted Nurse Jim standing by the admissions desk.

"Tenney!" he said with a grin. "Good timing—we're just getting set up."

I smiled, but winced inwardly, grateful that he didn't say anything about Logan being there. I introduced everyone as we followed Jim to the Gathering Place.

We approached the door, and I looked nervously at Mason. He gave my shoulder a squeeze. *You've got this,* his eyes told me.

Here goes nothing, I thought as I led the group inside. Nurse Jim had set up the space for our show, moving the chairs and couches into rows and clearing a space at the front for Logan and me.

Otherwise the room was empty except for one person: Logan.

He sat tuning Alice's guitar under a large banner that had been strung from the ceiling. Its hand-painted glittery letters spelled out WELCOME, TENNEY & LOGAN!

"Logan!" Aubrey shrieked, and dodged through the maze of chairs to hug him.

My parents looked startled. Logan just waved, still unaware that my parents had doubts about him.

"Alice has been talking about Tenney and Logan nonstop," Nurse Jim said. "All the kids are excited for the concert, so they painted the banner to welcome you two. Some of these kids have serious medical situations," he continued gravely, "so we're grateful for anything that can help make them feel better."

"So are we," I said.

My parents looked at Logan and back to me, bewildered.

"I'm sorry," Mom said to Jim, "I don't know—"

THE GATHERING PLACE

"How to thank you!" Mason interrupted with a smooth smile. "This is fantastic. We're really excited."

Mom and Dad looked even more confused.

Luckily, Jim didn't seem to notice. "Great!" he said. "Now if you'll excuse me, I need to help wrangle our audience," he said, and slipped out.

I took a deep breath and faced my parents. Dad was already frowning. "What's going on?" he asked. "You said you were playing a solo acoustic set."

"I never actually said it was solo," I corrected gently. "I *am* playing an acoustic set, but as it turns out, Logan's also playing one at the same time. With me."

I flashed my biggest, brightest smile at my parents, willing them to understand. Their faces remained stony. Before anyone could say anything, Aubrey dragged Logan over to us, chattering about how happy she was that we were playing together again.

"Logan said he'll play with me for the last song, too!" she beamed. "Isn't that a great idea?"

"I think so," I said, glancing at my parents.

TENNEY SHARES THE STAGE

They didn't say anything.

Just then, Portia stuck her head in. "Tenney, there you are!" she said to me. Zane and Ellie were behind her.

It seemed like everyone saw one another at exactly the same moment. Logan's jaw dropped, and Portia let out a surprised laugh, and Zane's face got all squinty, like he thought he was seeing things.

"What the heck? What's going on?" Zane asked.

I tried to answer, but everyone started talking at once, trying to figure out who knew what. It got even worse when Logan's mom and brother arrived. I tried to break in, but no one paid any attention, the storm of voices getting louder and louder. Finally, I stood up on a chair and waved my arms wildly, until people saw me and quieted down.

"Thank you," I said, taking a deep breath. Everyone's eyes were on me, waiting for an explanation.

"I want to apologize to all of you for not sharing the full details about what's going on," I said, "but I didn't know how to make this concert happen without doing that."

THE GATHERING PLACE

I turned to Zane and my parents. "I know you
don't think Logan and I should be playing together
right now, but over the last few weeks, I've realized
that he's as much a part of my music as I am." I
took a deep breath. "Also, even though I didn't ask
for permission, Mom did say I was allowed to jam
with Logan sometime," I pointed out. "Just think
of this as 'sometime,'" I added lightly.

My parents didn't look amused, so I turned
to Logan's mom. "Mrs. Everett, I know you think
Logan's too overwhelmed to play music, but I think
it's everything except music that's stressing him
out. Music is what makes him happy."

I looked at Portia. "You were right when you
said Logan and I had to trust each other. That was
really hard for me. But now, I can't imagine not
sharing my music with Logan. I trust him, and he
makes my songs better."

Finally, I turned to Logan, who was watching
me with wary eyes. "I'm really, really, *really* sorry
that I didn't tell you I invited everyone to this,"
I told him. "The truth is, I wanted to play this
concert with you, but I knew you wouldn't have

done it if you thought I was trying to get you to reconsider our partnership."

"You're right, I wouldn't have," Logan said.

"But will you now?" I asked.

Logan remained silent, his eyes guarded.

I sat down in the chair, suddenly exhausted. This wasn't going well at all. Everybody seemed so angry—mostly at me.

Just when I was about to give up hope, Mason spoke. "I'd just like to remind everyone that although Tenney and I have been mildly deceptive, this concert is for an extremely good cause." He looked at my parents. "For that reason, I seriously hope we won't get grounded," he finished.

Dad rolled his eyes, but cracked a smile.

"We *did* say Tenney could jam with Logan sometime," Mom reminded him.

Dad broke into a frustrated laugh, but smiled, too. "Yeah, yeah, I remember," he said. "Unfortunately."

We heard a flurry of giggles behind us as Nurse Jim started leading in a line of kids.

"Looks like it's too late to cancel the concert,"

THE GATHERING PLACE

Portia said. "Besides, we wouldn't want all of Mason and Tenney's secret planning to go to waste."

"True," Zane admitted.

"No, we wouldn't," Logan's mom said, wiping a tear from her eye.

Kids were streaming into the room now. Some were teenagers, a few were as young as five. All of them wore blue-and-white hospital gowns along with their own colorful pajama bottoms and slippers.

Amid the crowd, I glanced at Logan. I couldn't tell what he was thinking, and it made me nervous.

"So what do you want to do?" I asked him.

"I think ... we should warm up," he said slowly.

And as a half smile broke across his face, I had to hug him.

The next few minutes were a flurry of activity. Jaya and Holliday arrived wearing homemade Tenney & Logan T-shirts and helped keep the kids entertained while Aubrey, Logan, and I warmed up. Mason and Dad set up our sound equipment, and Mom and Mrs. Everett talked to Zane, Ellie, and Portia.

I spotted a nurse helping Alice navigate her

TENNEY SHARES THE STAGE

oxygen tank around the sea of chairs to a seat that
Logan had saved her in the front row. Seeing Logan
and me, she brightened. I smiled and gave her a
little wave.

Finally, the microphones were set up and we
were ready to start. Aubrey drew in her breath
with a sharp, scared noise.

"Don't worry," I said, giving her a squeeze.
"You'll do great."

"Definitely," Logan agreed. "They're just
kids—like us—remember?"

Aubrey nodded, but as she sat down in the
front row with her accordion, her face looked pale.

Logan and I stepped up behind our microphones, and the crowd of kids started cheering.

"You ready?" I murmured to Logan.

He nodded, fingers twitching along his guitar
frets. "I'm nervous," he whispered.

"You shouldn't be," I replied. "We're in this
together."

"Right," Logan said, and in that moment
I knew he believed it.

HEALING MUSIC

Chapter 15

I had never been more ready for a show than I was now. I flipped on my microphone, took a deep breath, and kicked off our show.

"Hi there," I said to the audience. "I'm Tenney Grant, and this is Logan Everett."

"And we are Tenney and Logan," Logan said.

I threw a surprised glance at him. He grinned.

"Or Logan and Tenney," I added. The audience laughed, but Logan nodded at me. *It doesn't matter which name comes first,* his look seemed to say.

"We're here to play some music for you," Logan told the audience.

I nodded. "Music makes us feel better and stronger when we listen to it," I said, "and it helps us heal when we're sad or frightened. For us, the best way to heal from anything is doing what we

love," I continued, nodding at Portia. "And what
we love is music. We hope that in some small way,
our music makes you feel better, too."

I focused on my guitar, my fingers gliding
along the frets into position.

I glanced at Logan, counted off with four slaps
on my guitar, and we jumped into our first song,
"Reach the Sky." It's catchy and upbeat, and Alice's
favorite, which made it the perfect way to start our
set. As my hands danced across my guitar strings,
I could feel energy stirring in the room. Some kids
clapped along to Logan's bouncy rhythm guitar as
I played the jangling melody. Alice sang along for
the entire song, and when we finished, she stood up
clapping wildly, her cheeks rosy.

"Thanks," I said into the microphone and
beamed at her. "That one was for Alice. If it weren't
for her, Logan and I wouldn't be here today."

Alice grinned, turning bright pink.

Without missing a beat, my fingers picked out
the intro to "Where You Are" as Logan joined in.
Although we'd planned our set list during our video
chats, we'd only rehearsed the one time at Dad's

shop. Normally that would make me nervous, but somehow I didn't care how perfectly we performed. I just cared that we were up there together.

As it turned out, it was one of our best performances ever. As Logan and I played, we'd check in with each other, exchanging a look at the end of a line or between songs. When I'd first started performing with Logan, he'd point out my mistakes and I'd get angry. Now, though, we helped each other whenever one of us messed up. When I hit an off note, he gave me a nod that said *keep going*. When he started to rush, I played my chords at the right tempo a little louder, and he adjusted. We still made mistakes, but overall our show went smoothly because we were looking out for each other. We trusted that we were both trying to make the music the best it could be.

Finally, it came time to play "The Nerve."

"This is a song about when you work with someone and they start to annoy you," Logan said into his microphone.

I laughed. "It's also about how sometimes you can be friends with someone but also get frustrated because they're so stubborn, like Logan."

"Or because they're a perfectionist, like Tenney," Logan said with a grin.

The audience laughed.

"This song's also about how important it is to build trust," I said, locking my eyes onto Logan's. "Because that's what makes true friends."

"Like us," Logan said, and I could hear the trust in his voice.

The first half of the song flew by in a beautiful, fizzy dream. It felt like I was floating as we played our duet for the first time in front of Zane, Portia, and the rest of the room. When we reached the third verse, we began alternating lines.

"You're always changing track like a scattered hurricane," I sang.

Logan took the next line. "You don't know how to let things go or how to take the blame."

"You focus on the bad when you should celebrate the good."

"Your sunny attitude boils the blood in my veins."

"And it seems like I'm the only one that's trying here," we harmonized.

HEALING MUSIC

As the music streamed through us, I thought of all the things that had happened to get us to this moment. It hadn't been easy, but it had been worth it.

Finally, it was time for the ending chorus, my favorite part of the song:

> 'Cause we strike a nerve,
> The one that makes the hairs stand on your skin
> When we are heard
> Together we have so much more to give
>
> 'Cause it's for music
> So I guess we do this
>
> You're a pair of infuriating
> Crazy maddening, always nagging
> Shoulders to stand on
> Let's meet this head-on
> I'll let you get on my last nerve

Logan and I snapped to a crisp end and grinned at each other. The crowd erupted in applause.

"Thank you," I said.

When the audience settled, I glanced at Aubrey. It was time for her to play with us, but she didn't look excited. Her face was a whitish-green, and she was gripping her accordion like it was a life preserver.

"For this last song, we'd like to bring up someone we think is really talented," Logan said. "Aubrey Grant, who plays a mean accordion."

Aubrey walked over stiffly and stood next to me. As I moved my mic over so we could share it, I noticed her fingertips were trembling on her accordion's buttons. I reached out and touched her hand.

"Don't worry," I whispered. "We've got you."

"Yeah," Logan said from her other side.

"Okay," Aubrey said, breathing in. Her face relaxed, and her hands settled.

"This is a new song called 'Someone Who Believes,'" I told the audience. "It's about those scary moments when you feel like you're alone . . ." I said, looking at Logan.

" . . . And you just need a reminder that there are people out there who have faith in you," Logan added,

HEALING MUSIC

smiling at me and giving Aubrey a little nudge.

I counted off, and we started the song. As we played through the first verse and chorus, Aubrey fumbled her keys a few times, but Logan and I were always there to catch her. We slowed when she got off-tempo, and sped up when she rushed from nerves. By the end of the first chorus, our guitars had blended with her accordion's melody into a wave of sound holding us all up.

I looked at my parents, Zane, and Portia, who were standing against the wall at the back of the room. As we started into the second verse, I sang directly to them:

I know that getting there's not easy
We'll never know unless we try
If we just give up all that we love
We'll let the moment pass us by

When we reached the bridge, we quieted our instruments. For a moment, it seemed as if the earth had stopped spinning. Then Logan and I sang in harmony to a silent room.

TENNEY SHARES THE STAGE

"This is, this is our dream," we belted. "We will, we will believe." We repeated the lines once more, our voices getting stronger with every note.

As Aubrey joined in on the final chorus, the room was electric.

This is my favorite part of playing music, I thought. *The way everyone comes together to make it great.*

The last notes sounded, and the room filled with applause. Aubrey's eyes sparkled brighter than her glittery dress as she took her bow between me and Logan. Then she hugged me, our instruments clunking together softly as she whispered, "Thank you." I squeezed her tighter.

When I stepped back, I was surrounded by familiar faces—Mason and my parents, Jaya and Holliday, Mrs. Everett and Jude, Portia, and Ellie—all talking and laughing with love in their eyes. Happiness overwhelmed me. For a moment, I thought I might cry, but instead I took a deep breath and thanked everyone.

I looked over and saw that Alice was talking to Logan. As I joined them, she gave a little joyful hop, and we hugged.

HEALING MUSIC

"Thank you so much for playing," Alice said.

"Thank *you*," I said. "Without you, none of this could have happened."

Someone tapped me on the shoulder, and I turned around. It was Zane.

"Do you two have a minute?" he said to Logan and me. "Someone wants to talk to you."

We followed him out the doors, up some stairs, and around a corner to an alcove, where a young woman sat gazing out a window. As she looked up, I realized it was Belle Starr.

"Belle!" I said. "You came!"

"Your set was fantastic!" Belle said to us, jumping to her feet.

"Wait . . . you were here the whole time?" I asked, confused.

"Of course! You invited me, remember?" she said with a mischievous smile. "I slipped in and stood in the back after you started your first song."

"I didn't think you'd actually show up," I blurted.

Belle laughed. "What can I say? I'm a fan," she replied. "What are y'all doing after this?"

TENNEY SHARES THE STAGE

It turned out we were going for barbecue.
Zane took us all to his favorite spot, called Smiley's,
with sawdust on the floor and ceilings as high as a
barn roof. As I walked inside the restaurant, I felt
as light as a bubble, like I could float up into the
rafters any second. Even after I loaded up my plate
with pork ribs, corn on the cob, and biscuits, I still
felt like I could fly. Now that the concert was over,
my worries were gone, too.

Our group sat at a long table and filled the
place with noise. Logan and I chatted with Mason,
Jaya, and Holliday, and Aubrey sat next to her idol,
Belle Starr, taking a million selfies. Then a blue-
grass band started playing a rough-and-tumble
tune, and we all went wild dancing. I whirled so
fast around the makeshift dance floor that I finally
got dizzy, and I had to sit down.

My parents and Logan's mom were deep in
conversation with Zane, Ellie, Portia, and Belle.
After the waitress picked up our dishes, I thought

we were all going home, but Belle stood up with Zane at the head of the table.

"I want to say a little something to Tenney and Logan," she began, her gaze shifting over to us. "Y'all really inspired me today, not only with your music but with the way you handled your audience," she continued. "You didn't have to play that concert, but I could tell you wanted those kids to get a chance to hear live music. As I watched them, I could tell they didn't just love the music, they *needed* it. And that gave me an idea."

Belle leaned forward, her bright blue eyes sparkling like sapphires. "I've been thinking about doing a big concert here in Nashville later this summer, after my world tour is over," she continued. "I could donate most of the proceeds to this hospital. What do you think?"

"I think that's a great idea!" Logan declared with fire in his eyes.

"You could play an acoustic show for the kids at the hospital, too," I suggested, and Logan nodded.

"Okay," Belle replied. "So we could visit hospitals during the day and do the big concert that night. What do you think?"

She looked at us expectantly, and so did Zane.

"What do you mean?" I asked, suddenly confused.

"I mean, what do you two think about being my opening act?" Belle asked.

I'm fairly sure I forgot to breathe for at least thirty seconds. Belle performed at huge arenas in front of tens of thousands of fans. I couldn't believe what I was hearing.

"Your opening act? At a big concert here in Nashville?" I croaked.

"Yep!" said Belle with a radiant smile.

I forced myself to inhale. My heart felt like a pinwheel, spinning in excitement as my thoughts scattered in a million directions. I looked at my smiling parents, who seemed to be okay with this plan. But when I turned to Logan beside me, he looked devastated. That brought me back to earth.

"I don't think we can," I said. "We're not supposed to be performing together."

"We've been talking about that, actually," Zane

said, glancing at my parents and Logan's mom.

"We all agree that we may have underestimated the bond you two have," Dad said lightly.

"Not to mention how powerful you two are onstage together," Portia added.

Logan and I looked at each other, hopeful and confused.

"So what does that mean?" he asked.

"It means that we think you guys should continue to play together," Mrs. Everett told him.

"Really?" I yelped.

Zane nodded. "I haven't voided your contract, so we can pick up right where we left off, working on original music," he said with a grin. "Only we'll just add this concert in. What do you say?"

"It sounds amazing!" I said, thrilled.

Then I glanced at Logan. His expression was a shifting mix of emotions.

Logan might not want to rejoin the band if his mom needs help with Jude, I realized. And I wasn't going to say yes without him.

"I don't know what to say," Logan said finally. "I have a lot of other responsibilities."

TENNEY SHARES THE STAGE

"We know," Portia noted. "We've been talking about that, too."

"We thought you and Jude could start coming to the shop after school on a regular basis," Dad told Logan. "That way, you and Tenney can practice."

"Right, and I can help watch Aubrey and Jude," said Mason.

"No! *I'll* watch Jude, and you can watch *me*," Aubrey told him, putting her arm around Jude protectively.

Logan looked a little overwhelmed. "Y'all would really do all this? Why?" he asked.

"Because," Mason said. "We believe in you guys. If we can help, we want to."

"I can help, too!" Holliday proclaimed. "If you need a backup, I'm available for babysitting."

"So am I!" Jaya added.

"But we're going to have to rehearse a ton and—" Logan began.

"We'll keep right on helping," Dad said firmly. "It'll be the summer, so school's out. Jude can hang out in the shop all day if his mom chooses."

Aubrey's eyes lit up. "We can have music

camp! I'll teach you how to play cowbell and accordion," she told Jude, who looked excited.

"And y'all can come on over for Sunday supper anytime," Mom said to Mrs. Everett.

"We would love that," Logan's mom replied.

Zane tipped his porkpie hat back on his head. "Don't forget that Tenney and Logan will get paid for performing with Belle," he pointed out. "So that should help, too."

Logan sat down on a bench, and I sat next to him, a little dazed.

Belle smiled at us. "So? What's the verdict?" she asked, putting a hand on her hip.

Logan opened his mouth, then closed it again, looking at me.

"I'm in if Tenney's in," he said. "We're a team."

Suddenly, everyone's eyes were on me.

"Tenney? What do you say?" Belle asked.

It took me a moment to find my voice, but when I did, I spoke out loud and clear.

"Yes!" I said.

We were going to open for Belle Starr!

SONG LYRICS

The Nerve

by Alaina Stacey

Tenney:
I don't like the way you shrug
like you've got nothing else to say
And I don't like the way you always
want to do it your way
You turn around and do
exactly what I ask you not to
And I can feel you criticizing
every move I make

And it seems like I'm the only one
that's trying here

Logan:
I don't like the way you think
that you know all there is to know
I don't like the way you think
you're better all on your own

★ ★

I turn around and do
exactly what I need to do
'Cause you're always moving
just a little bit too slow

And it seems like I'm the only one
that's trying here

Chorus:
You've got the nerve
to act like I'm the one
who makes this hard
It makes me hurt
to think that we might
mess this up
And I'm done letting you
I can't get through to you

Let's meet this head-on
I'll let you get on my last nerve

Tenney: You're always changing track
like a scattered hurricane
Logan: You don't know how to let things go
or how to take the blame

Tenney: You focus on the bad
when you should celebrate the good
Logan: Your sunny attitude
boils the blood in my veins

Tenney and Logan:
And it seems like I'm the only one that's trying here

Chorus:
You've got the nerve
to act like I'm the one
who makes this hard
It makes me hurt
to think that we might
mess this up
And I'm done letting you
I can't get through to you

Let's meet this head-on
I'll let you get on my last nerve

Instrumental Break

Ending Chorus:
'Cause we strike a nerve
The one that makes
the hairs stand on your skin
When we are heard
Together we have
so much more to give

'Cause it's for music
So I guess we do this

You're a pair of infuriating,
crazy maddening, always nagging
shoulders to stand on
Let's meet this head-on
I'll let you get on my last nerve

Someone Who Believes

by Haley Greene

Pen and paper in my hand
Just so you can understand
I believe we have a voice
I believe we have a song
The stage is right where we belong
The stage is right where we belong

Chorus:
I am chasing this dream of mine
I just need
Someone who believes
Someone who believes

Verse 2:
I know that getting there's not easy
We'll never know unless we try
If we just give up all that we love
We'll let the moment pass us by
We'll let the moment pass us by

Chorus:
I am chasing this dream of mine
I just need
Someone who believes
Someone who believes

Bridge:
This is, this is my dream
I will, I will believe
This is, this is my dream
I will, I will believe
This is, this is my dream
I will, I will, I will, I will
Believe

Chorus:
I am chasing this dream of mine
I just need
Someone who believes
Someone who believes

ABOUT THE SONGWRITERS

ALAINA STACEY was born into a family of musicians and learned to sing before she could talk. She grew up in Chicago but moved to Nashville to build her career as a singer-songwriter. Despite her early success, the road to Nashville hasn't always been easy. "It's really hard to hear no in this business, but unfortunately it's very common," Alaina says. "When it first happens, it's really disappointing and makes you want to quit." Then she found that rejection can be "a blessing in disguise, because you learn things about yourself as an artist and what you need to work on that help you move forward."

Her favorite thing about performing is getting to share her music. As she puts it, "Performing before an audience gives you an energy you don't get when you're just singing songs in your bedroom!"

Just as Tenney found inspiration through her frustration with Logan, Alaina finds inspiration in strong emotions and "the way songwriting transforms difficult emotions into something beautiful." About the song "The Nerve," she says, "It was easy to write because I was able to pull from the emotions Tenney and Logan were feeling in the story and imagine what they might write for each other."

HALEY GREENE got her first guitar in middle school and started picking up chords on her own because she wanted to join a band. She also plays piano, and she now performs regularly around her college town and has put out a CD as well.

"I just love the communal atmosphere of performing," says Haley. The first time she heard people singing her own lyrics back to her during a performance was "one of the most incredible experiences I've ever had. I feel like I'm just one with the crowd." For Haley, that's what being a performer is all about, not money or fame.

As a girl, Haley, now twenty-one, lived in China, Africa, and Ecuador, where she attended high school and started performing. "Just being exposed to all these different musical styles really helped influence the direction I wanted to take and my identity as a musician," she says.

While writing "Someone Who Believes," Haley identified strongly with Tenney's character. "She feels intimidated by the talent around her. As the storyline goes on, you can see her growing confidence. And confidence is really the key to being successful in music. I really related to that!"

SPECIAL THANKS

With gratitude to manuscript consultant
Erika Wollam Nichols for her insights and
knowledge of Nashville's music industry;
to music director Denise Stiff for guiding
song development; and to songwriters
Alaina Stacey and Haley Greene
for helping Tenney and Logan
find their perfect harmony.

ABOUT THE AUTHOR

As a young reader, Kellen Hertz loved L. Frank Baum's Wizard of Oz series. But since the job of Princess of Oz was already taken, she decided to become an author. Alas, her unfinished first novel was lost in a sea of library books on the floor of her room, forcing her to seek other employment. Since then, Kellen has worked as a screenwriter, television producer, bookseller, and congressional staffer. She made her triumphant return to novel writing when she coauthored *Lea and Camila* with Lisa Yee before diving into the Tenney series for American Girl.

Kellen lives with her husband and
their son in Los Angeles.

Parents, request a FREE catalogue at
americangirl.com/catalogue.

Sign up at **americangirl.com/email**
to receive the latest news and exclusive offers.

READY FOR AN ENCORE?

VISIT

americangirl.com

for Tenney's world

OF BOOKS, APPS, GAMES, QUIZZES, *activities,* AND MORE!